Father Luke's Journey into Darkness

Father Luke's Journey into Darkness

St. Ignatius of Loyola and the Catholic Sexual Abuse Crisis

Nancy Carol James

Foreword by William Bradley Roberts

WIPF & STOCK · Eugene, Oregon

FATHER LUKE'S JOURNEY INTO DARKNESS
St. Ignatius of Loyola and the Catholic Sexual Abuse Crisis

Wipf & Stock
An Imprint of Wipf and Stock Publishers
199 W. 8th Ave., Suite 3
Eugene, OR 97401

www.wipfandstock.com

PAPERBACK ISBN: 978-1-5326-5045-1
HARDCOVER ISBN: 978-1-5326-5046-8
EBOOK ISBN: 978-1-5326-5047-5

Manufactured in the U.S.A.   MAY 17, 2019

Dedicated to all those who have suffered sexual abuse during the Catholic sexual abuse crisis.

Contents

Foreword

The sex abuse scandal of the Roman Catholic Church is a tragedy for all concerned. Nobody has derived benefit from it, because everybody is diminished. Even those who claim enmity with the Roman Catholic Church must forgo *Schadenfreude*—gloating over the misfortune of others—because nobody can honestly hold him or herself apart, as if, "This has nothing to do with me." Such a statement is untrue and self-deceptive. Other ecclesiastical bodies—Protestant, Orthodox, independent—would be naïve to try to place themselves above the scandal or to rejoice in the suffering of the Church of Rome, because the issue touches all churches. One reason this is true is that people outside Christendom do not scrutinize the details of the crisis long enough to pinpoint the responsibility. No, blame is spread wide, because many people paint communities of faith in one broad swath.

John Donne declared, "No [one] is an island entire of itself; every [one] is a piece of the continent; a part of the main . . ." What diminishes one diminishes all. Many people are furious at the entire church universal because of the issue of sexual abuse. Two examples will bear this out: It was recently reported that priests in England are frequently insulted by strangers in public, based on nothing other than the wearing of a clerical collar. Two causes of this behavior can be cited: the increasing secularization of the culture, and the scandal of sexual impropriety, especially that involving minors. The second example is that of a clergy friend who, while riding an elevator with one other passenger, was shocked when that person suddenly spat on him, calling him a pedophile. Never mind that the clerical collar he was wearing was Anglican in style, not Catholic. To his angry assailant, the difference was negligible. One collared cleric was no better than another; all were equally stained.

Of course, sexual abuse by clergy, while widespread in the Catholic Church, is not limited to that denomination. In Canada, whole dioceses have gone broke because of financial settlements to the families of First Nation children, who, having been placed in institutions, were abused by Anglican clergy. Even Southern Baptists, who preach such stringent moral rectitude, have been marred by clergy sex abuse.

Crimes involving children, however, seem to evoke the greater wrath of society, and no wonder. While abused adults often have some recourse or some means of defense, children usually do not, and so are especially vulnerable.

What causes adults to assume that harming children—whether sexually or otherwise—is tolerable? What creates an environment that provides opportunity for such behavior? What causes the adult psyche to rationalize sexual abuse? What allows clergy—shamans of their culture, who in many instances are beloved for their otherwise beneficent, sacrificial acts of kindness—to undergo such a Jekyll and Hyde transformation? Such questions must be addressed with serious clinical inquiry and not through hasty speculation.

In the meantime, the public's primary impetus is for control, not for clearer understanding. Society wants the behavior stopped, then understood, not the other way around. In addition, the lives of those abused need to be rescued, the damage addressed, and the wounds healed, so that something approaching a normal life is achievable. As for the perpetrators, the culture cries out for immediate cessation of the abuse and for punishment. The outcry is for emergency triage more than for systemic change.

That instinct is totally understandable. But what next? How is abuse stopped? How would systemic change look? How do we cure the underlying causes of sexually abusive behavior? How can the environment be changed so that opportunity for abuse is denied? And then, though little sympathy is left for them at the end of the day, what happens to the lives of the perpetrators once intervention has halted their behavior? Is there any redemption for them? These are questions that beg long-range solutions.

What about the condition of celibacy? No doubt some people, called to such a state for religious reasons, are able to fulfill their vows. But for others, celibacy is demanded of them in order to earn the right to practice the vocation to which they are called. Celibacy in these cases is not a vow taken willingly or joyfully, but a behavior imposed upon them. Does this create a burden that provokes errant behavior? Laying aside genital expressions of sexuality, what are the broader needs for human warmth and companionship? Are physical acts of tenderness and compassion, expressions of love, needed for health and happiness?

These are some of the complex issues raised by Nancy Carol James's gripping novel, *Father Luke's Journey Into Darkness*. Previously, the Rev. Dr. James has handled the genre of memoir (*Standing in the Whirlwind*) and numerous works of theology, biography, and biblical studies (various studies of, and translations of the writings of Madame Jeanne Guyon, the seventeenth/eighteenth-century French mystic). Now showing herself to be a skilled storyteller, Dr. James delves into the sensitive and controversial area of clergy abuse. In her capable hands, fiction is shown to be an effective way to approach some of the complex questions raised above. Caught up in the drama of her story, we are impelled to deal with the issues not so much in scientific, clinical ways (as important as those are), but in the manner they present themselves in the actual world: as events that shape and direct the lives of real people.

THE REV. WILLIAM BRADLEY ROBERTS, DMA
Virginia Theological Seminary (Episcopal)
Alexandria, Virginia.

Acknowledgements

I wish to thank all the many courageous priests and laypeople who tried to stop the Catholic sexual abuse crisis. They have inspired me to write this fictitious story about this horrific time in our history. The places in this novel are true, while the characters are an artistic creation.

I also thank Melora and Hannah James for their assistance with research and art creations. I thank Roger Nebel who helped with the research for this book. I thank the Rev. Bill Roberts wrote the introduction for this novel.

During my PhD dissertation research, I researched at the Vatican library and I thank all of those who made this possible.

List of Characters

Oscar: Homeless singing man

Bishop Daniel Cahill: Bishop of Washington, DC

Monsignor Peter: Rector at St. Charles Parish, Washington, DC

Father Luke: Assistant priest at St. Charles Parish

Father Jerry: Italian priest at St. Charles Parish studying to be a Jesuit priest

Hannah Bigelow: Church administrator at St. Charles Parish

Sister Clotilde: Nun at St. Charles Parish

Father Bruce: Diocesan priest in small parish in Washington, DC

Father Hudson: Rector of large Roman Catholic Church in Washington, DC

Rev. Dr. David Sanchez: Vatican Canon lawyer

The priest dressed himself: snug dark blue T-shirt, Levi jeans, and a red Nationals baseball cap partially pulled down over his face. Calling his contact in the diocese, he heard again the plans.

"Two of them for all of us. Tonight in northeast Washington, DC at Stanton Park in the playground area. At our magic midnight."

"How much?" he asked.

"Five hundred. Your discretionary fund has plenty. I will meet you later."

The priest paused. "There is no harm in this, right? Only occasionally do I get to do this."

His acquaintance heard the pleading tone of voice and answered with words of comfort, "Of course not, Father. I will hear your confession tomorrow morning. And these enthusiastic workers get some needed money."

Relieved, he hung up and started planning for the rendezvous so near the Capitol Building—both sex and power involved with this evening. And now with a few anticipatory drinks, the priest began his frivolities.

Late that evening, he entered one of the six gates leading into the circular park lined by cherry blossom trees with tiny buds. He walked past the central statue of Revolutionary War hero Nathaniel Green on his horse with his upraised arm pointing energetically toward the playground. The priest's goal? The playground jungle gym with its large, raised platform. This playful atmosphere, surrounded by safety walls, concealed and allowing a happy view of the stars. Who would have thought of such a perfect place for a party? A discreet city park, surrounded by green boxwoods and pink flowers, full of memories of happy and innocent children.

Then he saw her, a young Hispanic girl with long beautiful dark hair standing outside the gate. The priest walked up behind her and without a word began stroking her. Screaming, her terror brought running friends. In a blazing second, even through his drunken haze, the cleric realized his mistake.

Quickly two men swung their fists at him. Blow after blow rained upon the drunken priest. Then a man rode his bicycle from the opposite end of Stanton Park. Dressed entirely in solemn black, the letters on his t-shirt announced US Capitol Police.

"The police! Let's get out of here!" one said. They dropped the beaten man near the playground equipment. The priest faintly heard the shocked eruption, "That's the priest at my family's church!" Then only running footsteps filled the air.

Dazed, the priest blacked out, while the unnoticing policeman calmly cycled past him.

Soon the pummeled cleric heard the faint sound of humming in his ear. Then an old spiritual song clearly emerged, "My Lord, what a morning, when the stars begin to fall!"

Opening his eyes, he saw a well-known man, Oscar, smiling and singing to him. Wincing, the priest looked at his growing bruises and felt his aching head.

Then reaching his cell phone, he pressed the speed dial.

"May day. Beaten up in the park."

"What happened?"

"Hurry!"

Soon a tall man entered the playground.

"Can you walk?"

"Some."

"Let's get out of here. We'll say strep throat in isolation until you heal. Your face looks bad."

Chapter One

What happens when a priest falls? They have reached up, hoping to touch God and move into heaven, hoping against hope that they will find the gracious gift of endless ecstasy and join the family of saints— the Church Triumphant. Yet this long spiritual journey contains tests and trials. Some fall.

Priests had kept generations of the Roman Catholic faithful at St. Charles Parish in Washington, DC. Veering between issues of faith and politics, three priests from the Society of the Cross led this unusual flock. The Marines of the Catholic Church, their community offered both intellectual rigor and personal piety.

Their motto suited them: "All for the greater glory of God."

Their boys' Catholic school produced some scholars that later attended Georgetown University, located so close to the parish, prominently placed on a hill in this vibrant city.

Monsignor Peter Dawkins led this parish. On this spring day, Peter weeded the red tulip beds with a local man they called Oscar Hammerstein. Hats shading their eyes, they looked as if they were caring for the original Garden of Eden. Oscar sang as he gardened, "This little light of mine! I'm goin' let it shine!"

This unusual homeless character could speak no words, probably due to a stroke. To communicate he sang lots of spirituals and folk songs. His charm opened many doors. He seemed to know every popular song ever written. Peter gave him a small room on the first floor of the parish rectory, announcing to Oscar, "Our bishop's church needs your protection."

Today Peter chatted with Oscar. "What a beautiful day in this early spring!" Hannah, the church administrator, walked by, dressed in a business suit and talking on her cell phone. Oscar sang to her, "All things bright and beautiful, all creatures great and small, the Lord God made them all!"

Smiling, she waved.

Hearing these jovial sounds, another priest, Father Jerry, walked out, bearing from his kitchen small cups of espresso on a tray. He placed them on a bench next to the giant replica of the Roman sculpture of the Capitoline wolf, the giant mother wolf guarding her human twins, Romulus and Remus.

Trailing behind Jerry, Father Luke questioned him. "Now that we have a Jesuit pope, shouldn't we do Saint Ignatius's *Spiritual Exercises*? We read Teresa of Avila last Lent."

Jerry raised his hand, as if to exclaim in Italian, *Splendido!*

Seeing Oscar, Luke smiled and the homeless singer bowed in response, his face covered with instant rows of symmetrical wrinkles.

"Each little flower that opens?" he warbled, questioning, pointing to the aphids on the rose bushes.

Peter looked. "My mom taught me a way to stop those." Using his elbow, he wiped the sweat off his face. "Hey, let's go eat."

In the rectory kitchen, Peter placed a huge bowl of tapioca pudding in front of Oscar who immediately sang, "Rejoice, rejoice, believers!"

Peter sat down to read the *Washington Post* while Oscar enjoyed his treat.

A headline read, "Night Vandalism in Stanton Park." Peter casually scanned the page. The short article read, "An unusual circular symbol was carved in an old cherry blossom tree, and in the children's area park, a puddle of blood was found near the playground equipment. Anyone with information about this is asked to contact the DC Metropolitan Police." Luke walked in and instantly Oscar warbled back, "Let us break bread together!"

Three priests from different backgrounds shared quarters in this Victorian mansion. Monsignor Peter ruled the roost. In his mid-forties, his attractive dark-blonde hair and blue eyes helped his entertaining sermons. A similar age to Peter, the brown-haired, short Father Luke Murphy was the perpetual assistant. His mystical love of God brought him this luxurious position, though his lack of connections ended chances of promotion into the hierarchy.

The younger and darker Father Jerry Golino, descended from a long line of Italian priests, added a touch of the noble heritage of Rome.

This tribe of priests slept in their individual rooms located on different floors. The singing Oscar slept as a security guard with Luke next to him in a spacious room. The privileged Jerry resided in the front second-floor and Peter reigned from a master bedroom suite at the back.

Father Jerry, a chef trained in Italy, nurtured others with his culinary creations. "Come on over!" Jerry would say, and the parishioners happily responded. The parish enjoyed new tastes: ripe radichio and unusual pasta creations reveling alongside nut-encrusted fish. And soon he would walk in bearing some flaming dessert, fire dancing with excitement.

After pasta and expresso, Jerry would begin the conversation. "The blood of the martyrs is the seed of the church." He explained that the sacrifices of the faithful brought renewed life to the Body of Christ and at times, a remnant caused rebirth. "Teresa of Avila and John of the Cross helped save the church in the 1500s." Hearing his words, the faithful gained rich passion in their late-night conversations.

And who would want to miss the spiritual feast Jerry made? He regaled them with rich tales of Rome, the city nurtured by Romulus and Remus, the children nurtured by the great she-wolf. Jerry had insisted on putting an imitation of the Capitoline wolf outside their home and everyone who walked by reacted with an instinctive respect to the great historical masterpiece. In the courtyard stood a giant she-wolf, forehead frowning, ears moving forward, standing head ready to swing any direction, with hanging breasts and nipples dripping sweet milk. Underneath played the baby sons, reaching, ready to nurse, smiling. They trusted in their caring world. The folklore of Rome said that these two twins, Remus and Romulus, founded Rome and the magnificent Roman Empire that later birthed the young Christian faith.

This February evening, St. Charles Parish celebrated Mardi Gras before the beginning of Lent. At the red doors, Peter stood welcoming them.

"More chocolate cake, Annette?" he said to the middle-aged woman, plate in hand. "You've outdone yourself—as always! I can't hold myself back from this."

Annette flushed. "I make it only for you, Father." She placed it on the crowded table.

A teenaged boy walked by with two small boys following him. "You're not a pied piper, are you?" Annette called out. "Hey—we need to get ready for when you play the Easter Bunny!"

The kids danced in a circle chanting, "More candy! More candy!"

The boy smiled and then quietly added. "Later. I promise." Then, "Hey, Father Peter, the bishop's here."

And true to the boy's word, processing through the gardens, came the purple-clad bishop surrounded by a group of handsome, laughing priests. The gregarious Bishop Daniel Cahill liked so many parts of God's good creation: shrimp and lobster, Nationals baseball games, Redskins football, elaborate worship services, the political concerns of the Catholic Church, talking to those at the White House and Congress. Everybody loved this affable and fun bishop–such a charming face for the traditional Christian faith.

Today he chatted. "Good fathers, it is all about a healthy dependence on God, the Church as the body of Christ, with our beloved Pope Francis as its head. And you, my brother priests, are so important to Christ's body."

Walking in, Bishop Cahill threw his arm about Peter. "Great job here! This parish is popping with new life and fun in our special church. And our Lord will bless you for your work and so will I. In fact, I am placing my special envoy here, Father Leo, to connect your programs with our influential colleagues in Rome. You know I have great plans for you." The bishop faced Peter directly with a small wink that only Peter could see. The bishop continued softly, "Recently Leo came from his home at the Vatican and he is here to pump up our programs some. Let's talk later."

Peter nodded affirmatively and then his voice floated over the crowd to greet an incoming parishioner. "General Knight, how good of you to come! Have you been to Afghanistan lately?"

With a curt yes, and a firm handshake, the military leader swept into the room with his wife following closely.

Then a DC official walked in and Peter was ready. "Mayor, what a great DC renaissance you are leading! What you are doing for our city is wonderful!" Then softly he added, "And how is the security for the International Monetary Fund meeting coming? I know this has to be a headache for you."

The mayor nodded yes and added jovially, "All in good time!" Parishioners swarmed around him, asking questions about the growing prosperity of their city.

Playing a more moderate role than the affable Peter, Father Luke walked around greeting and talking. Some clergy called this working the crowds, yet Luke understood that his pastoral presence grounded this frivolous reception. He heard from concerned people about a bad medical test or a relationship problem or perhaps even about God.

Luke loved these momentary but spiritual conversations: is it possible to relate to the living Holiness we call God? But if truth were told, Luke enjoyed coming out of his introverted life to this active group of people. These parishioners achieved much in society but never ventured much into the spiritual realm. But in his studies in Rome, Luke had focused on the great mystic Saint Ignatius of Loyola, who founded the Jesuit order and influenced Luke's Society of the Cross. Luke frequently quoted a line from Ignatius.

> May Our Lady intercede between us poor sinners and her Son and Lord; may she obtain for us the grace that,

with the cooperation of our own toil and effort, our weak and sorry spirits may be made strong and joyful in his praise.[1]

This church work is a good balance, he had said to himself on more than one occasion. Some of his professors, though, believed that Luke had put his light under a bushel because he should be teaching or living as a mystic monk in interior seclusion. But no, Father Luke supported the gregarious Peter in his work, while enjoying this front-line engagement with highly successful people.

Luke listened to a conversation about a local idiosyncrasy. The doctor regaled, "Why do they have police on bicycles in Washington? Reminds me of a different era when the main problems in DC were growling dogs and a boatman on the Potomac River who had had a few too many Guinness Stouts." For indeed the Washington DC police sat squarely on their bicycles looking more like kids masquerading as the arm of the law than real authorities. The doctor continued, "What do you do when you arrest someone? Insist they balance on the seat with you while you struggle towards a car somewhere. "Hold on while we pump. Don't squeeze me too tight or we will fall!""

An older woman laughed, "Sometimes you can see a whole crowd of policeman practicing on their bicycles in parking lots, teetering around orange cones as they train for quick turns on streets." Everyone smiled in recognition of the ways of the DC police.

Now Peter walked up to the parish hall stage, climbed a few stairs, and over to the waiting microphone. "I am so glad that you have come to our Mardi Gras gala on this Shrove Tuesday! Look at all the wonderful treats we have here—so many thanks to our chefs! I am sure that we can indulge tonight and come to confession tomorrow. We will have extra time available to forgive you for whatever you do tonight, won't we, Father Luke?" Flushing, Luke waved his hand in agreement.

---

1. Ignatius of Loyola, *Spiritual Exercises*, 327.

Peter continued, "Lent is upon us starting tomorrow, folks, with its prayer, fasting, and almsgiving. This Christian practice began centuries ago to prepare to baptize or to renew their baptism at Easter. We are thankful for our Jesuit Pope Francis and pleased with our endeavors this Lent. We might not see many changes in ourselves, but God will be pleased. Yet we can't leave here without talking about money, can we? We have to give Caesar his due and our building does need some work this year." He ordered the waiting janitor, "Open the curtains to see our new capital campaign goals for St. Charles!"

As the curtains drew apart, the relaxed crowd saw the teenager preparing to unveil the drawn thermometer on a poster board. Peter raised his voice and called out, "Thanks for helping with our little kids!"

Then Peter continued. "The goal this year is one hundred thousand dollars for our new air conditioning system. That will be nothing from us, though, because God blesses our finances and gives us everything we need." The attuned crowd shook their heads in agreement. "And this year, I want us to give a special gift to Bishop Cahill: such a great leader we are blessed with! Do you know what our good bishop said to me: "Peter, your parish is the best one in DC. Now that I am close to retiring from this divine burden of being a bishop, I might just give you a run for your money and take the parish for myself!"" Laughter interrupted Father Peter's talk. He continued. "But enough said: eat, dance, enjoy! You have come to the best party in Washington, DC."

Standing in the crowd, Luke heard the laughter as if from a distance with his head spinning. He reached for the wall to hold himself up: were his springtime allergies acting up already? An inner ominous thunder persisted. Instinctively he looked out the window, only to see the same cherry blossom trees with their delicate, unopened buds, yet the vast skies shone with not a dark cloud in sight. Luke put down his plate and shakily walked towards the door. Maybe he had better have a moment of quiet.

"Is something wrong, Father?"

Looking up, he saw the church administrator, Hannah. "Just a little dizzy."

Putting down the microphone, Peter headed for the dinner buffet adorned with warm chafing dishes supporting alluring fish creations and warm cherry cobblers. Balancing her full wine glass, the red-haired Annette stopped him. "Monsignor, did you get to go on the bishop's winter Caribbean cruise?"

"I would not have missed it." Then smiling, "As a monsignor I was invited. For those priests who stayed behind to fill in, we prayed a blessing for them."

"Oh, Father, you are too much!"

"Enjoy yourself, my dear. This is a night to remember."

Intent now, she added, "My son, Father, he needs to be confirmed." Looking down, she said, "Andrew is doing so well in school and now with confirmation, everything will be great for him. Father, he has scored tops on his SAT scores and is good in basketball also. Hard to believe he is my son!"

"And we must celebrate also! Bring him directly to my office and I'll take care of this for you. Bishop Cahill leads a great confirmation service and has one coming up soon. His new assistant Father Leo will educate our children."

She looked directly into his grey-blue eyes.

"My dear Annette, maybe you could come by tomorrow afternoon. We could have a little sherry and talk about all the good going on in your life."

He clasped her hand closely and then moved closer to the table with the well-dressed people chatting everywhere.

That night, Luke had the same nightmare he had suffered for several months. They started in the same way. Howling sounds came from a mysterious mountain: the tall steep peaks covered with dense curly green vegetation with not a sign of life anywhere except beneath the bizarre plants. But from the underbrush emanated scratching and long painful howls: then an even more painful silence. Night after night of howls from an unseen source.

Howls reaching out, echoing in oddly blue skies, starting low and then reaching high to tense warbling, crying out what: the end of something? A warning?

Luke woke up again, desperately sitting up, wanting to charge away from here to be anywhere else. All he knew was danger. Opening his eyes he saw his clerical shirts hanging calmly in the closet and his Bible where he left it on his nightstand.

Luke knew the bizarre message. The human race had lost the will to survive. Luke understood the human race was in danger of annihilation. "So much suffering everywhere!" he murmured to himself. He remembered that Pope Francis had written that "We have come to see ourselves as lords and masters, entitled to plunder her at will."[2] And he knew the truth that plundering happened everywhere.

And Luke also knew that other howling forces felt this ultimate lack, mourning, moaning, and warning humanity.[3]

2. Francis, "On Care for our Common Home."

3. Central Italian fifteenth or sixteenth century (Possibly Roman fifteenth or sixteenth century), *The Capitoline Wolf Suckling Romulus and Remus*, National Gallery of Art, Samuel H. Kress Collection.

Chapter Two

What happens when a priest falls? Bishop's hands had been on his head, praying for the power of the Holy Spirit. And when priests' hands reach out in destruction to others, the spirit worlds collide and evil grows and flourishes, all covered by the name of Holiness.

In the dark of the night, the priest, dressed entirely in black, walked by the closed Washington DC Convention Center, then looking both ways, walked to the side of the Andrew Carnegie Library to the hidden place under the immense, old tree. There he exercised a secret ritual. Taking out a vial of warm blood, he poured it on his hands and rubbed his wet hands through his arm, saying "Moloch! Moloch!" He waited and soon his glassy eyes spun wildly around, looking intently at each passerby. He knew now what to do.

Leaving as furtively as he arrived, in a rush of satisfaction, the priest thrust his tightly clasped fists over his head. He took out the Vatican knife. He stepped back, raised the knife over his head and swishing it down, hit the tree, tearing the bark open and revealing the tree's tender interior. Sap ran out everywhere. He twisted and turned the knife, mutilating the bark in six different directions until the shape of a pinwheel hung on the surface like graffiti announcing chaos.

At the church home on Ash Wednesday, Oscar sang the day in with "Morning has Broken!" followed by the thump against the door of the thrown *Washington Post* with a small headline reading, "Another Park Defacement."

The television in the corner droned on with the popular TV newscaster Gordon Peterson announcing, "More park vandalism occurred last night. In Mount Vernon Place Park, three oddly-shaped pinwheels with a circular wound were slashed in the hundred-year old oak tree. Horticulturists say that the bark has been penetrated and the tree might not survive. The police chief asks for help from the DC citizens for solving these continuing acts of vandalism. This makes the second park defacement."

This news announcer was not the only one concerned about the mutilated trees.

The female police chief picked up the phone and called the mayor.

"This is not a major crime in our city with our problem of increasing numbers of murders, but I want to let you know that another tree has been defaced in a park with an odd pinwheel symbol. My forestry people say it might kill the tree."

The mayor listened.

"But what concerns me are our cherry blossom trees. There was a half-done slash in one cherry blossom tree in Stanton Park and that tree recently died. It looks like someone lunges like hell at these trees, gashing and slashing. Rumors are spreading everywhere that there are occult activities in the parks."

The mayor sighed. "In the wake of the sniper murders, now a tree-killer, right before our Cherry Blossom festival and that stressful International Monetary Fund meeting. If this gets out, it might hurt our popular festival."

The chief of police continued, "It's spooking people. And sometimes there is unexplained blood. Rumors are spreading everywhere people are getting attacked in our parks." She paused.

"And it might escalate. We don't know the thinking of this kook. The symbol looks like two peace symbols on top of each other but it might have more meaning. It is like Zorro, a symbol done in extravagance and style. We don't need any stylish killers here."

The mayor spoke firmly. "Pull out all the stops to get this solved. Stop the bad publicity right before the IMF meeting."

The following day after his hospital visiting, Luke had a command meeting at the Vatican embassy in DC, close to St. Charles Parish and the official residence of the US Vice President. Sighing, he noted the waving yellow-and white Vatican flag with two keys criss-crossing one another, one silver key of the world and the gold key to heaven.

In front of this embassy on Massachusetts Avenue NW, the lithe, gray-haired man stood on the front sidewalk for his long days of work. Not the gardener or the sexton, this man carried his signs that read, "Pedophiles work here" and on the flipside his message read, "Corrupt leaders!" Luke skirted carefully around this odd man thinking that of course a few rotten characters had gotten into the priesthood, but some bad apples can happen anywhere. The old guy stood looking around him, occasionally returning any friendly waves from passing cars. Suddenly the man turned towards Luke with a firm opening statement.

"I don't listen to nuns who hit my hands with rulers."

This appealed to Luke's humor as he too remembered a few aimed taps by his own nun teachers. He smiled, "None of us liked it. You got my sympathy there." Then a little louder he added, "But I got a good education."

The committed man shook his head, "I don't need anyone to order me around."

Luke started walking away, yet the man leaned toward him, in an insistent voice, "You don't need this bishop telling you what to do."

Flashing through Luke's mind were seminary memories of some dull lectures but balanced by the vibrant faith of others. Stunned that even for second he had agreed with this oddball, Luke stopped and responded, "I wish you well." Even as he said it, he checked to see no one had overheard him. What would Bishop Cahill think about him even talking to this man? The bishop had declared this old guy a lunatic. The church had unsuccessfully tried through every legal means to deprive him of the Constitution's First Amendment rights and banish him from this public sidewalk.

Luke knocked on the front door. As the butler admitted Luke to the required meeting, the man went back to yelling at passing cars, "This Catholic Church hides pedophiles!"

Luke stopped to look out the window at the strange man while worrying again about these meetings at the embassy. Why he was required to come? He knew the official story. The Roman Catholic Church with its shortage of priests understood that the remaining priests needed support. Even after the wild 1960s, many priests still renounced their ordination vows. So some bishops had decided to give the priests a chance to work on their relationships and hired therapists to lead the groups. Using a convenient location, Luke's group met at the DC Vatican headquarters in a spacious, secluded room in the back of the building. The priests sat on comfortable, golden-brown couches as they faced another hour of required conversation.

The priests discussed personal issues, yet worried, Were they being spied upon? Were they open, partially open, or blowing them out of the water with our confrontations? More and more of the priests fit into the latter category.

Coming in late, Father Luke sat next to Jerry, who spoke. "To me, the problem is competition between priests. I think this is because our church has lost some of its strong Roman spiritual foundation."

The young, red-haired Father Bruce spoke up, "I agree! We can't speak openly in this diocese anymore. If I say something critical, will this comment make it back to the bishop? Then soon I'll be transferred to some rural parish with hours of driving every day. Or even sent to Alaska!" The other priests murmured in agreement.

The friendly therapist, Dr. Wagner, intervened. "I guarantee you, Bruce, I will not break your confidences and speak to the hierarchical bishops and cardinals. I only report some general ideas about what we think about problems, so the church becomes more hospitable to priests."

Jerry spoke out, "You are not the one we fear. The bishop has one of his generals here." Jerry had forgotten to change the language that the priests used among themselves. Flushing, he added, "I mean, of course, we have one here who has a future vocation to the episcopate."

This distinguished priest, Father Hudson from a wealthy and aristocratic background, quickly changed the subject. "We are all praying for the right bishops and cardinals."

This sparked some quickly-fired remarks about their lives from the red-haired Bruce again. "The bishop needs to help me with my schedule." He added, "We are dropping like flies!"

"I agree," Jerry concluded. "We are a needy group now. It didn't use to be this way."

Bruce continued pushing. "But the church seems to be struggling now, maybe even dying. There are problems inside with clergy leaving, parishioners aging, and the young disappear, even after they are confirmed. Of course we are all on edge."

Then in an almost inaudible voice, Hudson spoke out, "What is going on at St. Charles, Jerry?" Luke thought, *why ask him and not me?*

Jerry slowly answered, "We have a growing school and a large acolyte program. Many different boys now serve at the altar with us."

Hudson persisted. "I heard a wild story of a teenage boy walking around followed by some of the kids. And other stories also."

Jerry said slowly, "I'll tell you what I know. An older acolyte started volunteering in the childcare room. Last month, he was stopped by a parish usher as he was taking a three-year-old boy away into an off-limits area." The priests stared at Jerry, who paused and continued. "Monsignor Peter investigated and found out that the acolyte didn't know the rules about being alone with young kids. He said he was only emotionally fond of this child." Jerry ended lamely. "So I think the situation is resolved and over."

No one dared a response.

Soon the group stopped for the day and the weary, black-clad priests found their way back to their churches.

Hannah sat at her desk going through piles of paper. Seeing Luke, she began quickly. "On April 26, you have an invitation to Bishop Cahill's for a reception." Luke looked at his feet briefly with the odd thought springing into his mind, *You don't need this bishop telling you what to do.* "Please decline. I am busy that evening." Without another word, he and Jerry walked into the monsignor's office where Father Peter sat behind his desk. Peter briefly looked up but then quickly focused on the task.

Peter began, "We're dividing up the schedule of masses now. Are you ready?"

Without a word, Luke took his calendar out of his pocket. The priests scattered into distant chairs with the setting sun creating shadows over their faces. Lines of variegated light slowly moved across the red Oriental rug on the floor.

Peter spoke, "Now we are looking at Lent heading to Easter. Luke, you will do the noon day masses Monday, Wednesday, and Friday." He added, "You can enjoy your Sunday mornings off. Jerry and I will take the morning masses and you do the Saturday 5 p.m. ones."

Luke looked down intently at the calendar.

The silence deepened.

"If that is what you want, Monsignor."

Luke walked quickly upstairs.

In his room, he reached for his rosary beads and hoped for that inner vibrancy that came when he prayed. Now though, the beads seemed to lay flat and powerless in his hands as if they were martyred. Where was spiritual vitality? No more Sunday mornings? He would miss the parishioners and the community events.

"Darn it," he whispered. "I don't even know what is going on here."

After a sleepless night, Luke rose at 5 a.m. and sat at the church office computer to print up the Scriptures for his noonday service. Knowing Peter was out for the day, Luke made himself comfortable in front of the computer and suddenly a pop-up ad with a scantily dressed couple jumped on the screen with a jarring headline announcing, "Hot men! Slutty women!" Luke quickly jerked the mouse around, desperately trying to make it go away, yet every time he thought he had successfully disabled this, the nearly naked woman appeared again. As soon as 9 a.m. rolled around, Luke called the diocesan computer services.

That same afternoon, the diocesan computer tech guy sporting blue jeans and a brown ponytail arrived. "There is one thing you can try yourself that may help stop these pop-ups. With Internet Explorer open, choose Tools, Internet Options." He continued rattling off this information as he jotted notes for Luke. "At the top of the dialog box change your home page to Use Blank. Click OK, close IE and reopen to see if your home page is now just blank. If that works, then go back to Tools, Internet Options, and in the middle of the dialog box choose in order: Delete Cookies, Delete Files, and then Clear History. That may well clean everything up."

Luke stared at him. Then clearing his voice, he asked quietly, "What in the world are you talking about?"

Reaching for his bag of tools, the young guy stood up. Eyes averted, he said, "Getting rid of the problems related to X-rated websites." He stammered. "Look, it's tough to be alone." Then bolting for the door, he added, "I won't tell the diocese. They don't ever do anything about this anyway. Call me if this doesn't work. Just leave me a message saying that the spam has come back. I'll know what it means." Slamming the door behind him, he left, with a trail of questions in his wake.

Luke sat stunned. X-rated websites? Pop-ups? The only pop-ups he read about in seminary were demons popping up to tempt St. Antony, the father of monasticism, when the monk, celibate and fasting, lived in the rural caves of Alexandria, Egypt. Antony said to focus more on God when distracting temptations arise. Yet still Luke sat slumped over: what is going on here?

Upstairs Jerry approached his desk, his one place of luxury, to work on his PhD dissertation. Hoping to be a Jesuit, Jerry's passion for Roman mythology led to this half-finished degree from Georgetown University. He wrote about the Roman Empire and especially Romulus and Remus raised by their mother wolf. As he frequently did, he looked out of his window to see the statue of the mother wolf sitting out front.

Today Jerry took out paper. The words flowed quickly about the mythical founder of Rome, the generous she-wolf tenderly caring for the babies while protecting from predators. A wolf-mother bringing ferocious protection and eternal love! Wolves symbolized the glory of ancient Rome, as well as the Jesuit Ignatius of Loyola who had wolves in his coat of arms. Soon, Jerry hoped, these images would come out in academic terms for his PhD dissertation. Springing up for his afternoon hospital visits, Jerry began to whistle an old Gregorian chant, Veni Spiritus, *Come, Holy Spirit.*

As Jerry sprinted toward the door, he almost ran into Hannah. Quickly she blurted, "Would you come help me pick up the reception food for tonight's meeting?"

Jerry smiled. "Not today. Late for a prayer before a heart operation at Georgetown University Hospital." Suddenly he added, "Ask Luke!" As her startled eyes met Jerry's happy ones, Hannah heard a small "I can do it" from the priests' office where Luke sat.

Hannah added slowly, "Okay." After a pause, "I want to grab a sandwich first and maybe you are hungry also." Luke swallowed hard, nodding yes.

She explained, "I know you are busy, but I won't ever find a parking space around the caterer and if we both go, I can double-park and you can quickly run in to get it."

He trailed after her, head down. Soon walking into the local Five Guys restaurant, they were greeted by red-and-white signs announcing that the potatoes were from Hatch Farms in Warden, Washington. Fifty-pound bags of potatoes lay against the side wall.

Ordering her grilled cheese sandwich, Hannah murmured to Luke, "The best French fries in Washington!"

Sitting at the white glossy table, Luke peeked across at the blonde woman. "Hey, wasn't that latest park crime near here?"

"Yes, Mount Vernon Place, an historic park. Odd pinwheels cut into trees with dripping blood. Done at midnight. They taunt the authorities with these public ceremonies. With the new convention center right there, it seems odd to choose that for a crime." She added with surprise. "Always something in this powerful city! Who do you think is doing this?"

Luke thought back to his studies. "Sounds like one of those weird worshiping groups. Who knows? I took some classes at Loyola and we studied cults that get involved with things like trances and things like that. Could be they are sacrificing animals."

Then he said quietly, as he thought of a story to share, "When I took a Religious Studies class at Loyola University, I would drive up to Baltimore once a week."

"That's quite a long hike."

He smiled and nodded. "I used to go through a drive-thru mid-way and have coffee. There was a drought. Everything was dry and brown. The person in the car in front of me threw a lighted cigarette butt out of his window."

Hannah looked at him with puzzled green eyes.

Luke continued. "A small bush caught fire. The intercom lady asked me if I wanted to add a milkshake to my order. I said, "A bush has caught on fire here." She responded, "I don't understand you." I begged her, "The bush is on fire and flames are starting. You need to bring a hose to put out the fire." I heard, "Please, sir, just give me your order.""

Hannah started to smile.

Becoming alive, Luke laughed. "So I cupped my hands, like a megaphone and yelled. *"Come quick. Big Fire!"*"

Hannah leaned forward.

Luke quickened his pace. "The next thing I see is a woman peeking around the corner. She sees the now blazing bush and yells, "Get the hoses!" Soon fire trucks roar up and soak the bush. Later the manager hands me the largest cup of coffee I had ever seen. "It's free today!" he said."

Laughing, their hands bumped as they both reached for a French fry.

Hannah retorted. "Shouldn't you be encouraging burning bushes rather than drowning them?"

"Yes!"

Then swallowing, he abruptly added, "Do you notice anything odd at St. Charles?"

She looked at her Timex watch. "Father, I need to get back with the food for that meeting. Let me think about that one."

At the next therapy meeting, Luke noticed that when he sat down, other priests seemed reluctant to sit next to him. His years in the church had taught him that probably someone gossiped about him.

After a brief opening prayer, Father Hudson began to talk. "The diocese always had a mix of priests. When I was a new priest, the clergy was divided about where you came from."

Bruce agreed. "Now most of the division is between those who acknowledge that we are overworked and those who deny this."

Reacting, Hudson said, "Some of our priests sow the seeds of discontent. Negativism."

Jerry fueled the flying sparks. "A few years ago they named monsignors and divided us even more. We had no monsignors for thirty-seven years." This comment sparked Luke to think, "Why Peter instead of me? And why any monsignors at all?"

Than Bruce blurted out in fiery frustration, "Oh, come on! If all we think about is our position, we've become superficial."

Luke sat back. When he was ordained, he expected a group of men dedicated to God and community; he would stand united with them in love. And what had he found? A group of men divided over anything: background, titles, and the bishop. Friendship in this climate was tough. And maybe that caused the first part of the journey into darkness that many priests take. The minute after the ordination vows were taken, everything began to break apart. Was there a united, fraternal brotherhood and even a moment when the vision of Saint Ignatius was alive and truly flourishing?

On a darkened March night after a Saturday evening service, Luke walked into the church. Stopping suddenly, Luke saw mid-way up the first flight of stairs a tall figure standing with his long slender arms outstretched toward him. The shadows hid his mysterious face and yet the dancing light clothed him in a long gown of shiny silver luminescence with only darkness where the face should be. Hamlet's ghost has come to warn me, Luke immediately thought. Outstretched bony, trembling fingers with open palms facing upwards reached out to him, imploring and begging. The ghastly fingers tried again and again to breach the gap to touch Luke, but were stopped. The hands pleaded for help and the dark, hidden face bespoke a visit from the underworld. Trembling, Luke reached for the light switch, the ghost was gone yet vestiges of an ancient terror gripped him.

"It's dry," Luke heard in a strangulated voice. The janitor Carlos was coming down the stairs, his pale face panting in an asthmatic attack. Luke quickly said, "Can I help?"

"I've already taken my medicine. It's dry. Do you notice?"

"Yes, it's everywhere."

Luke slumped down and then said all he could think of. "We all feel it." Luke grimaced. "I don't understand what is happening here."

Shakily, Luke walked upstairs. The ghost had both begged and warned.

Chapter Three

What happens when a priest falls? The Body of Christ, so gravely wounded, hemorrhages in terror. The priest's soul had been flooded with grace, yet now he will find the grotesque and the bizarre. And when fallen priests meet committed ones, the monstrous meets the sublime and only God knows what will happen.

In a Washington, DC park, the priest looked at the two rivers flowing one into another. *Power,* he thought, *where the Potomac and Anacostia rivers join: the pure power of flowing river currents symbolizes the joining together of different worlds.*

All geniuses recognize places of power.

We'll claim this one now. What pure excitement, pleasure, and power.

And who do we have for this ceremony?

He called the official. "We are helping the market again. I ordered some from the Nationals game, just a mile from here."

Listening for a moment, he replied, "Yes, Buzzards Point. Not well known, but out of this world. You'll love it!"

Later in the mysterious dark of the night, he searched through his pocket and dug out a gold-colored knife emblazoned with the seal of the Vatican, two keys crossing each other. He took the caged hamster out of his back seat. He saw the men waiting and quickly grasped the animal by its neck and strode into the middle of the group. "Moloch! Moloch!" they prayed reverently. And soon the squeals of the animal with its dripping blood promised an answer from Moloch.

Then flicking his knife open, he chose the largest tree and approached it in reverence. He raised the knife up and with a quick gesture, penetrated the tree's thick bark, gashed a pinwheel and with worship-filled strength, encircled an open wound around the tree, whose sap immediately sprang forth from the deep wounding.

Now bring on the celebration; and with the advent of car headlights, he saw approaching people. Chaotic wildness visits the waiting mob.

Early the next morning, Jerry once again thought of the wolf and instantly upon reaching his desk felt new words. Wolves, and particularly the alpha male and female wolf, watched for predators and in an organized fashion fought back. Their hierarchical pack allowed them to fight off any threats to their young.

Jerry wondered, *how do wolves have the instinct for hierarchy?* To become alpha wolves, they were tested by winning a long and often brutal fight to prove their strength. After an alpha wolf took command, together he presented a formidable defense to any threat. Jerry thought of the beauty of the open pack loping along in the wilderness, yet the alpha male listened for howling communications from others.

But what thesis comes here? Jerry thought. All academic thought comes first in symbols, dreams, and poems. The way the wolves structure their lives was symbolic of the structure of community life. Where was the alpha wolf in their community? The bishop?

A brief flash of an image of a running, loping wolf in the wilderness shot through his mind. Majestic beauty! Passion!

Yet my pack, my community, is loping not for beauty but now fighting against the powers of darkness. Our pack is being destroyed wolf by wolf. We are all weakened.

Jerry knew he must have patience as he waited for answers.

But patience was in short quantity in Washington, DC.

The mayor called the DC Police Department and spoke directly, "What happened at the Buzzards Point Marina?"

The police chief tried to sound positive. "Look, we had police watching parks everywhere but what kind of nut would go to Buzzards Point with all of those secure facilities there?" She made an irritated noise. "With both the Coast Guard headquarters and the National Defense University right there? Security everywhere? Who would do this at that spot?"

The mayor leaned back. "Rats." This property was already a sore point with him. "And how did the military get that prime location anyway with the intersection of the Potomac and Anacostia Rivers? With all the development of the waterfront, I wonder if we could get this property back in the name of Native American history. You can almost see the hand-built canoes in those timeless rivers." In his mind he remembered the beautiful V shape of the waterways of these two powerful rivers connecting one with the other. "What did these criminals do?"

"Cut more pinwheels into a large tree right at Buzzards Point Marina. But what is puzzling is some unexplained blood splatters and bloodied clothes. I think there is violence or sexual assault going on, like cultic rituals."

The momentary peace the mayor had enjoyed disappeared stolen by a thief in the night. The IMF meeting was soon and the chief was telling him of odd spiritual rituals being conducted in public parks. Financial leaders from the world will live and play all over Washington, DC at the time of the Cherry Blossom Festival. And bizarre rituals are happening under the eagle eyes of security.

"Leaders of the entire world are going to be here and we can't stop some kooks from defacing trees with knives? Get this situation stopped! We will look like crazy Americans."

Late that day Luke overheard Peter's raised voice talking on the phone in the church office, "Chancellor, what do you mean a priest from this parish solicited men in a park? Or are you saying that a man from this parish solicited a priest?"

Luke walked more slowly now.

"Nonsense. We have two fine priests here, Luke and Jerry. They wouldn't do that."

The old air conditioning system clanged on and all that Luke heard was "any authorities."

Today Oscar's songs were dismal. He started with, "Nobody knows the trouble I've seen!" Father Luke bowed and Oscar responded, bowing, but he stayed bent over and low. Father Luke, leaning down, saw tears flowing from his eyes.

"Why, Oscar? What's wrong?" Oscar lifted his arm up and bowed with tears dripping down his face. Unable to offer any comfort to the disconsolate singer, Luke walked toward the 5 p.m. church service. As he got his key out, he wondered, what is it about a church in the evening? There was the quiet presence of the flickering flame from the red lamp stating that Jesus was present, body, blood, and soul. The divine was here. Yet also he sensed ominous presences: spirits of the dead, fiends hanging around to torment the faithful, hoping to inhabit an open human heart. The sense of the restless presence grew as Luke hung his purple priest's stole around his neck.

Luke walked up into the sanctuary. He saw the brown cross with Jesus's contorted body hung, his head leaning on his right shoulder, with the ancient words INRI whittled into the crude sign over his head. INRI: Jesus the Nazarene, the king of the Jews.

Flashing through Luke's mind came a memory from Kansas, a time in gym when Luke, the puniest kid in the class, got kicked in the stomach. Luke twisted in pain. The class bully leaned over him and said, "I'm sorry." He then leered as Luke rolled from side to side. Luke winced at the sight of Jesus's contorted body with nails tearing through his skin.

And then—out of the back of the darkened church, came the female voice, "How are you tonight?"

Jumping, he twisted his shoulder as if to deflect a blow. Looking around, he was relieved to see Hannah sitting in the back pew. Her long dark-blonde hair reached almost to her elbows and her face shone with alert energy. Her green eyes pierced into his.

His immediate response of "Fine" stopped mid-course. He looked and saw her bright eyes meeting his, waiting in hope for a real encounter. Breathing slowly, he walked past rows of empty pews where generations of worshipers had prayed. The souls of the faithful! Yet in spite of the soft red light glowing in the sanctuary, it seemed to be empty of love and faith. Now the consecrated church sanctuary seemed filthy, like a cluttered movie theater with littered sticky spilled soft drinks and empty popcorn bags. What are we watching here? Jesus on the cross looking for an encounter. Turning and waiting, for what?

Her voice penetrated his thoughts again. "What's going on here?"

The back doors were open; the already-lit red-flaming candles on the altar created an eerie glow. The white walls were broken by the stations of the cross exhibited in colorful stained glass windows.

Sighing, he sat next to her on the nineteenth-century brown church pews. "You know also?"

"Yes. The church is dying. There are signs everywhere."

Father Luke looked straight ahead, then a quote popped into his mind: "Our house is desolate."

In the echoing, empty church, he asked, "What do you see?"

"Crisis everywhere. No one talks. Ministries fail. Who can miss seeing that the church is struggling?"

The flaming candles on the altar sputtered and Luke leaned forward to hold his head in his hands. The sound of screeching tires outside broke the silence.

Softly, he began, "Our church computers had some problems. So I called in the tech guy from the diocese." The priest sat, shivering. Why am I cold all the time now? Then he leaned closer to Hannah, looking for any sort of enlightenment. "The man said, "Someone's going to X-rated sites and they are leaving bugs on the computers.""

Hannah's face turned to stone but she did not answer. The old building creaked.

Why am I telling this to her, Luke wondered. Then he knew the answer. Words rose out of the depths of his heart. I'm desperate. For the first time in my life, I feel utterly lost. And who can I trust?

He had attended the diocesan meetings for years. The bishop had his group of favorites and I'm not one of them. They thought he was irrelevant to take all of this devotion seriously. *Yet that is why I am here.* They taunted, "Take your place," like it was a performance.

"And they are trying to get rid of you, aren't they, Father?"

"I don't know but it sounds like you do." He paused. "I have been here for ten years."

"I can see it. I think one of the other priests is behind it."

Hannah continued, "Some boy keeps calling the voice mail. He screams, "The water's running! Please stop!""

Father Luke paused.

Hannah said very softly, "I think a criminal is on the loose here."

He nodded. "Watch and wait. Waiting is difficult but answers will come to us."

Then they heard footsteps coming up the side stairs. How long had this person been here? Had he heard? Or was it a spirit? Then the door swung open. His hair looking askew, Father Peter walked in, with an immense grin on his face. "I am so full of thanksgiving. I just came in to pray."

Quickly Hannah and Luke looked at each other. Luke sank back: could it be thanksgiving for over-hearing Luke confide in a woman about his personal fears?

Luke stood and briefly turning to Hannah said, "Will you stay for the mass and have a cup of tea after?"

She smiled, but quickly declined. "Not tonight. I'll see you on Saturday at our luncheon for the homeless." With a slight emphasis on the first word, she ended, "Wait for me then, Father."

Later at the Saturday evening mass, dressed in his purple chasuble, Luke looked out at the usual suspects. These churches in Washington, DC changed membership with every change in the president's administration. Yet tonight he saw a few that he recognized. The lovely woman Annette in the elegant hat. The officer, General Knight, who had taken responsibility for the parish records. And then, Luke saw him. That tall Vatican priest Leo, loaned now to the diocese, sitting in the back of his St. Charles parish.

The liturgy continued. Luke placed his hand over the bread. "He said the blessing, broke the bread, gave it to his disciples." Then Luke held the host high. "Take this all of you and eat of it for this is my body, which will be given up for you." Then hands shaking, he took the chalice, "Take this all of you and drink from it for this is the chalice of my blood, the blood of the new and eternal covenant, which will be poured out for you and for many for the forgiveness of sin. Do this in memory of me."

And then as Luke reached for the chalice, his hand hit it. As if in slow motion, he watched the gold chalice fall to its side and the wine splashed out in a circle of spreading blood swarming all over the pure white linen. Fiery red holiness crying out "Holy! Holy! Holy!" *Or maybe*, Luke thought, *this blood announces, the end of innocence.*

Following the service, Luke stood outside the main door greeting the waiting line of parishioners. Leo walked up and with complete eye contact announced himself. "You know I'm working for Bishop Cahill," Leo said, enunciating each word. This seemed as effective to Luke as starting a new Inquisition and he stared in return.

Leo continued, "I work in all the churches now. We are starting several new confirmation classes and hope to restructure the diocesan confirmation program. We want to keep the young confirmands active and involved." He walked rapidly away without acknowledging Luke's startled eyes.

The ghost's warning had struck home.

Jerry continued his solitary journey. Why would Ignatius use wolves as a symbol? Jerry thought of everything he knew about them. They lived in packs and they were incredibly committed one to another. To be part of the pack was to have a family and belong. To be part of the pack was to experience a shared structure of relationships that endured. To be part of the pack was to have the benefit of knowing that they look out for each other.

Jerry stared out his window. "Maybe that is what I want." He smiled. "I want what wolves have. A pack bringing strength, comfort, and adventure. I want to run and be part of the pack."

Early the next morning, Luke heard a soft knock on his personal door. His shiny black hair attractively combed, an alert Father Jerry stood there.

"Can we talk, Luke?"

All of Luke's usual excuses flooded into his mind but then he pushed them aside. He slowly opened the door. "Come in. Please?"

Jerry's face softened. He said, "Yes." Then he lifted up his arm to show Luke a white bag he carefully bore. "My cinnamon rolls, Luke. I know you like them. I also made my St. Bruno cream."

Luke stared. One of Jerry's specialties, this rare concoction consisted of a pudding made from sugar, eggs, and cream, then laced with strong coffee, becoming truly an adult delight. He heard echoing through his mind phrases from Jerry: "The eleventh-century Saint Bruno knew the rigors of monastic life and made this life sweeter with the goodness of custard." Luke poured the hot dessert-like beverage. "Please, Jerry, do sit by the window. I have had this room forever and the morning sun is delightful."

After Jerry offered the rolls on china plates, Luke found himself actually enjoying this. Could this be why they had those required group interactions? "Maybe we could do pizza next time," he said.

Then Jerry sat back. "I want to talk about your changed mass schedule, Luke. I know how unfair it is. It is amazing you carry on the way you do."

Luke's mouth fell open and then he swallowed and answered in a soft voice. "Thank you, Jerry. This has been very difficult."

Jerry lowered his voice. "I don't wish to hurt you, but you need to know some things. I can't tell you too much or we could both be destroyed." He leaned forward and began in a whisper. "Someone has it out for you. That seems obvious at this point but I can tell you are not watching and understanding the diocesan dance we all endure. Now we have a chief thug here, Leo, called the Queen Mother, who is trying to alert the authorities about you because one of his priest friends is in trouble. I'm not sure which one is in peril but you are the patsy here. I am not sure the community can save us from this destruction."

Outside a woodpecker began its rhythmic tapping.

Luke stared.

Jerry shook his head in disbelief. "You don't even know, do you? A priest solicited some woman in Stanton Park and her friends talked about it everywhere. Yet the men are here illegally—we call them undocumented now—and they refuse to go to the state authorities. St. Charles is all they keep saying. "The priest at St. Charles tried to have sex with me," is flying everywhere. The bishop wants a quiet end to this. They are trying to pin this on you."

Jerry continued, "Don't fall for trusting conversations with Cahill and Leo. Fight like hell here, Luke, or you may end up defrocked."

Luke started to ask who, what, how, and more but the other priest interrupted.

Jerry quickly answered, "I've told you more than I should. I don't know more details. I'll let you know if and when I find it out."

Luke paled. "What do I do?"

Jerry said, "We gave our lives to the church, all of us, and you surely don't deserve this. And don't think they don't realize that you are honoring your vows of celibacy. They don't do that. Your celibacy is the most offensive thing you can do."

Jerry's eyes looked out the window and then back at him directly.

"Our celibacy, though, gives us power to pray more fervently and listen more carefully. That's one reason the church asks us to be celibate. We need to use this power now. Our lives depend on it."

Jerry took another drink of strong coffee. "Beware, Luke. Living in this public house in this city full of Catholic parishioners, there is no privacy. If you need to talk, let's go to Shivi's Ice Cream on Wisconsin Ave after the meetings. It's always busy there and we can grab a few private words and enjoy ice cream at the same time."

Jerry looked at his feet. "This might be our only chance to know more about what God is really asking of us and to serve him more."

He walked quietly out, leaving his words of warning eating through the mystic Luke's soul.

Hannah heard the rapid footsteps of Luke quickly leaving the offices.

She thought, *We all want to leave this situation. But where do we go?*

Luke walked into the basilica, the Roman Catholic cathedral in northeast Washington, DC. He scanned the people: do I know anyone here? Do I look upset? Someone is trying to falsely accuse me. His thoughts tumbled together as he walked past the beautiful chapels lining both sides of the cathedral. Overhead the image of the resurrected Jesus Christ reigned.

Then he saw it: the chapel dedicated to the Virgin of Guadalupe with bouquets of white roses surrounding her gentle appearance. At the front of the chapel a young mother sat cradling a baby and watching over an active toddler. Was she crying? Why did she hide her face in the baby?

Luke walked toward the front altar. As he walked by the mom, he glanced to see if she wanted to talk but she showed no signal of wanting to interact.

"No cry, mommy! " The toddler reached for his mom.

Luke knelt in front of the altar and heartfelt words flooded his mind. "Mary, my Lady, I cannot go on. I cannot continue. This is too much."

He waited. All was now silence.

"I don't know what to say. As Ignatius says, I am a poor sinner but please send your Son to help."

Looking up, he saw sparkling light on the golden stars on the image of the Lady.

"Did you say that, Mary?"

Quiet.

"Did you say, *Go help my children*?"

From behind him, he now heard happy laughter from the toddler in the chapel.

"The bishop won't like this."

Luke looked up directly at the altar.

"Yes, my Lady."

Luke turned around to talk to the weeping woman. No one was there. Why didn't I hear them leave?

Go help my children.

As Luke walked silently into the rectory home, he remembered his passionate theology professor, David Sanchez, who had talked about evil as if he were in hand-to-hand combat with this power. This professor defined evil as the harming of human life. Evil parasitically attaches itself to good because it is not as strong as the good. People's sins of pride, power, selfishness, whatever they are, depend on goodness to support them.

Unlocking the front door of the church, Luke felt that now-familiar feeling of bizarre dry heat like a wall of hostility making the place threatening; the Bible calls these ugly forces spiritual principalities and powers.

Luke walked into the rectory library with the herald of Ignatius hung on the wall, a coat of arms with two gray wolves eating from the same pot, so very similar to the Capitoline wolf statue. Alert wolves everywhere! What an unusual symbol of wolves with lips pulled up, exposing huge bared teeth ready to attack, growling, tearing flesh off of living bones, ready to reveal the truth. Ignatius was a warrior ready to destroy any half-truth that stood in his way and he did it for the honor of his Lady Mary.

Luke looked for the book, *The Spiritual Exercises of St. Ignatius*. Opening the book, he saw an engraving by seventeenth-century Jesuit Herman Hugo showing a person's open heart with arrows shooting to God. "That's what I need," Luke muttered quickly. "A direct line to God!"

In seminary, Sanchez upheld this classic book as a means to discern the activity of spiritual forces and clarify one's own inner life. Let the hand-to-hand combat begin. Luke settled in a wood chair. "Stand up straight and fight for truth."

Luke now journeyed into the spiritual universe, remembering the words of Ignatius and claiming them for his own. Ignatius had suggested something like, "*Pray in the morning and evening. Keep a little, private notebook keeping a list of your spiritual life.*" Ignatius's signature ideas included, "*Overcome one's self without any tendency for disorder.*" Yet Ignatius respected privacy for the sinner except in the area of prostitution. Under the general heading of the Examen of Conscience in the Word, Saint Ignatius says, "*Don't make anyone else's private sins public except in cases such as public prostitution.*" *I get it,* Luke thought. In prostitution the person is victimized by being treated as an object, and that very act corrupts all humanity. And for the first time, in days, Luke felt real strength rising in his heart. Maybe he would survive this after all.

Like a good postmodern thinker, Ignatius said, use your imagination! Ignatius's Latin practically sang out. *Ut si per imaginatione cernamus anima nostrum.* Imagine situations to see where God is *in hac miserie valle*, in this valley of misery.

> When a contemplation of meditation is about something abstract and invisible, as in the present case about the sins, the composition will be to see in imagination and to consider my soul as imprisoned in this corruptible body, and my whole compound self as an exile in this valley [of tears] among brute animals.[1]

Understanding lusts as brute animals or beasts seemed right to Luke, who was still plagued by the deep primal fear of chaos, where humanity falls and loses the gift of the law and the prophets. Falling into depravity by losing the Scriptures, all humanity will drown in a murderous sludge of hatred. My soul, the part of me that lives for eternity, could be under the power of depraved and evil forces. Hence, I could live for eternity under the power of evil.

"Evil only has power if I cooperate with it. I won't do that. Let me go get that notebook." He headed toward Dupont Circle with its masses of energetic people, one of the city's night spot areas. Aglow with the bright sun, Luke walked past the circular park's fountain decorated by dancing nymphs and spurting water. Some lively men with dreadlocks played upside-down tubs, a woman teetered by on four-inch blue high-heels. The aroma of warm Krispy Kreme doughnuts floated in their direction. In the local pharmacy, a long line of restless men and women checked smart phones while waiting at the self-serve check-out, sighing, checking out the person next in line to see if he was moving fast enough. Dressed in his civilian clothes, Luke walked over to the spiral notebooks and rifled through them. Grabbing a red one, he walked over and took his place in the crowd of surging humanity and bought it. Pocketing the change, as he walked out, "Okay, Ignatius, I'll make my lists about what I know about God."

He sat down next a group of young men, their hair closely cut, adorned in tight jeans, talking while smoking cigarettes. For a split-second Luke thought, *I know a lot about God so this might*

---

1. Ignatius of Loyola, *Spiritual Exercises*, 136.

take a long time, but then he realized, *it's all second-hand. I can tell you what Thomas Aquinas thought, "All that I have written appears to me as much straw after the things that have been revealed to me." Or Blaise Pascal: "Fire! Fire! Fire, Not the God of the philosophers but the God of Abraham, Isaac, and Jacob." Or Jesus: "Blessed are the pure in heart, for they shall see God." But what do I know?*

1. The man who stands in front of the Vatican embassy said that I did not need this bishop telling me what to do. Was that a prophecy to me?

2. A ghost warned me and yet asked for my help through his outstretched hands. Warning me about what?

3. *Go help my children.*

Rigidly Luke sat with no more thoughts coming. *This is all I know after years in the church?*

A street vendor pulled his cart by with steaming hot dogs. Luke stood up, putting his notebook quickly in his pocket. That's all I know, he said. Maybe Jerry is right. This might be my only chance to find out something about God.

Arriving back at the rectory, Luke saw the hawk-eyed Sister Clotilde sitting at her desk, shuffling through papers.

"Father, what is the good news for today?"

Luke looked down, shuffling his feet.

"None," he muttered.

He started charging toward the stairs.

Clotilde stared at the disappearing priest. Maybe an outing or a picnic would cheer him up. They do have these organized priest groups now.

Reaching his room, Luke threw himself on the bed. *Help my children.* "How can I do that? I need so much help myself. And in this era of church problems, who can do anything?"

When studying at the Vatican, Luke had found many different kinds of people. Unwelcome in his mind was the knowledge of the long seminary showers Leo led with others, cavorting for hours. What did they call our house? The home of the Queen Mother, the scheming Leo.

Luke still remembered the evening in the seminary showers. As he walked out, Leo stood there naked and waiting, his thick hair pushed back from his cleansed face. Without a word he grabbed for Luke and tried to push him back into the private shower stall. Instinctively Luke pushed back and lost his balance, although in his shock his yell came out like a choking sound. All Luke could remember was falling on the wet floor and Leo, laughing, walked away taunting, "Another time then!" And Luke, grabbing his towel, ran to hit him and Leo had disappeared.

That day Luke thought about his choices. He could go report this sexual attack (it took him a while to acknowledge this term) to the seminary dean or even to the police. His Midwest roots yearned for this simple justice. Yet he knew that this form of justice would destroy him. The dean would look at him with superficial compassion, while realizing this could boomerang on him. Rumors would spread that Luke enticed this sexual encounter and then revengefully reported it. *Damaged goods, that Luke is,* would be said with shaking heads and judgmental looks. Some would talk of his feminine and weak beliefs (they had seen his heart-felt tears in chapel) and that he really wanted this. He might be sent home to Kansas surrounded by a spirit of failure.

So Luke swallowed this experience and locked it away. Now ordained, Luke still was pushing the experience down deep into his psyche, yet watching, always watching, to save others from this horrific episode.

But not all at St. Charles were praying. Alone this afternoon, Leo stood in his St. Charles office. He reached out for the Bible to check the Scripture readings for Sunday and then put it back on the shelf. He shuffled through the mail. As he walked over to look out the door, he stopped as if he heard something, then continued pacing. The required window in the office door opened out to a long hall leading down to the bathroom, with a toilet, a sink, and a blessedly large space between the sink and the door. Running water hid anything.

Yet now Leo heard another knock with the door shaking a bit. That blasted window the parish leaders had installed so that the priest was never alone had weakened the door some so now it bounced a bit when knocked. Yet these appointments were the harbinger of better things to come. Annette stood at his door with the familiar look of the overburdened mother.

Leo glanced in the mirror. With the same brown hair, his eyes seemed too small for his face. A few lines on his forehead gave him a seasoned appearance of wisdom. As he reached to open the door, he felt the usual sense of delicious expectation. How long would this hunt take? With one hand he swept up the prayer book and the other fingered his crucifix. After seating her in his office, he began the conversation.

"How can I help you, Mrs. DeSales?"

"It's my son, Andrew, Father. He needs to be confirmed and the monsignor said to enroll him in your class."

Perfect, Leo thought. "Yes, there's a new confirmation class coming up. I want to get to know the new generation and publish a research paper about how to involve them in our church. I will take a special interest in Andrew's class. I am sure he will fit right in, make new friends, and become confirmed in our church at the same time. And do make an appointment with our good monsignor for your own support. Our Holy Mother Church cares for everyone."

As the relieved mother stood up, the priest wondered whom to get to absolve him this time. He couldn't use most of the priests in this area now. His chest tightened.

He muttered to himself, "In fact, I can travel on a vacation to Rome and find a priest there for absolution. Let's have the fun first."

Yet what was that word that kept tapping away in his mind like a woodpecker: purity. He made a sudden hand motion. No one's pure. Where did that come from?

Annette dressed carefully the day of her meeting with Father Peter in a red and yellow flowered blouse under a black business suit. Looking from all sides in the mirror, she saw an attractive woman who might pass for a young aunt of Andrew. She ran out of the door and headed for her parish. Hearing her soft knock and arriving at the door dressed in his clerical blacks, Peter smiled at the sight of the well-groomed and beautiful woman. This will be a fun meeting.

"Come back here to my conversation spot," he said. In the corner, far away from all windows, he had put two comfortable brocaded chairs with pictures of beautiful eighteenth-century men and women on them, with the female sex sporting Parisian hats watched by the courting males. A small table with his rosary lying on it rested next to the comfortable chairs.

She looked down at her lap. "It's not really Andrew I wanted to talk about," she began, "It's me."

But Peter cut her words short with a beginning stroke and then a small comment, "What a beautiful red and yellow silk blouse." As he began to touch her, he added softly, "This will prepare you for your husband. We need to celebrate the years of service you have given your successful son!"

And many caresses and kisses later, the now wrinkled red and yellow blouse writhed like a coral snake in the grass, red touched yellow and yellow touched black. But what was that old saying about coral snakes: "Red touch yellow kill a fellow." And that wasn't even in the Bible, but her son Andrew was now in grave danger.

But she wasn't thinking about Andrew now, only her own rush toward satisfaction.

After the noonday mass, Luke headed over to the parish school to teach Latin. As he headed in the door, Luke groaned: the elderly sister, Sister Clotilde Kaluta sat at her desk, her chin-length gray hair carefully combed, her brown eagle eyes looking directly at everyone in the face, and her fingers with the care of a hungry vulture combing through backpacks looking for any contraband. She had seen these students, parents, and teachers all school year, yet checked everyone as if she guarded the pope himself.

The nun ordered, "Father, don't rush. The Holy Virgin says to magnify the Lord and not magnify your anxieties. It's not good for your heart."

Luke wondered yet again, when is this old woman going to leave here and torment someone in a community for retired nuns and sisters?

Clotilde continued, "Tell me the good word, Father."

What good word? A criminal on the loose and our security guard looks suspiciously at all the moms and dads she sees every day.

Reluctantly, Luke responded with the words of Ignatius, "*May Our Lady intercede between us poor sinners and her Son and Lord.*"

She eyed him and then slowly released him to enter, "Have a good class." Yet her eyes softened as she watched him leave. Why the peculiar burdened walk of Father Luke? The others didn't move like that—he looked like a daddy-long-legs trying to inch along and finding balance an elusive quality.

Then Clotilde continued, "Show me your ID please." Trying not to sigh too loudly, the dad put down his young son's Spiderman backpack and pulled out his driver's license.

Clotilde answered brusquely, "Move along."

Seventh-grade Andrew looked both ways after he left his literature class filled with uniformed young men talking of *Hamlet*, and walked toward the bathroom through school halls smelling of bleach. His father, the Foreign Service officer now stationed in the nation's capital, would kill him if he knew what had happened. It began in a meeting in Father Leo's office as he was studying to be confirmed. The class with eight teenagers went through lists of boring people from church history. At the end of one of the classes, Father Leo asked him to stay behind to talk about something.

The priest sat behind his official desk with his ordination certificate prominently displayed over his head and asked Andrew to come over. Then he turned on his computer and with the mouse clicked on a movie.

"Hey look at this, Andy!" No one called him that.

"But they don't have many clothes on. Is this a mistake?"

The monitor faced away from the door so people walking by could not see what was happening.

"Mistake? No."

The priest whispered, "Men later come back to thank me for showing this to them when they were your age. Great, isn't it?" Andrew didn't know whether to run, look away, or lean forward to see more.

Then the priest clicked the images off. "That's all for now. Stay again afterwards next week. I'll have more neat stuff to show you. This will complete your education."

Andrew walked out, hanging his dizzy head. Did this always happen in confirmation classes? Maybe the priests want you to know all about sex so that your education would be complete, kind of like an advanced physical education class. What would he do next week? Were all the kids doing this? Or was he the only and special one?

Reaching the boys bathroom, he washed his hands for the fourth time that day and headed back to his algebra class.

Chapter Four

What happens when a priest falls? Once he sought the Oneness of the Holy One and now he luxuriates in division and hatred. When a priest falls, all humanity suffers and corrupts.

In the darkened office, Hannah grabbed for the blinking light on the answering machine.

From the machine, a boy pleaded, "Please stop him. He said he was coming back to see me. Please. I can't leave my name. He's told me I can't talk about this!"

Hannah sat down at the desk, head in her hands. She had known people who talked to the Lord of all creation or maybe she had known people who had known people who had found this power. She needed this help desperately now.

Revealing her Baptist roots, she began, "Lord, I don't talk to you very often. Actually I have never talked to you before. But now, if you are there, I beg your gracious help." Was that a Sunday school phrase, she briefly wondered? "I have got to find the boy and I offer myself to you as your faithful servant, touched by the blood of the Lamb." That one was straight from her grandmother, the one who chose her Biblical name. "Help me find this boy and help him. In the name of Jesus Christ, our savior, Amen." That phrase was from the down-to-earth Baptist minister, wearing the same black suit every Sunday, you could see it in his eyes that having found both the pleasures and pain of the world, he had been there, done that, seen it all, yet felt that warm, ever-loving, ever-flowing blood helping him find his way through this darkness. Now bring that real blood into St. Charles, she prayed.

Hannah grabbed some papers as an excuse to walk into Monsignor Peter's office, that conclave of Roman elegance. She saw the priests' computer and saw that the email was up. *Never in my entire life have I done such a thing, even though I am responsible for all these computers. Maybe I should have been watching these all along.*

Now there is a boy begging for help out there. She looked at the Outlook Express with emails bearing only typical names about basic parish work. The altar guild drops by the communion bread. The treasurer pays for the furnace repairs. A priest writes about the spirituality of Saint Ignatius and wants feedback from his seminary friends. Then she saw a minimized website bearing the name "Hot X-rated" and she opened it. In front her shocked eyes, she saw a blurry picture of a boy in shadow, his wrinkled shirt framing his shadowed adolescent face. "Lord, have mercy!" She cried out. She felt hot liquid coming up her throat and, running to the bathroom, she vomited. Even as her breakfast flew out, she knew that now the Lord had consecrated her as a divine servant and baptized her by this horror. Something awful and dreadful is here.

"Oh, my God! That was a picture of a teenage boy."

Father Luke heard running feet downstairs and walked down to see. Hannah came out of the bathroom, her face breaking out in giant red, spreading blotches contrasting with her pale face emptied of blood.

"Miss Hannah," Luke began, "let me take you home. You are sick."

Hannah began to cry, but then stopped. A new servant of the Lord has strength, she decided. She looked into Luke's eyes. "Come see, Father. Come see."

They walked back into the office. Hannah took the door, shut and locked it.

"Brace yourself," and then the same picture of the scared boy flashed up.

Luke sat down and within a second walked over to the window, then back to the desk.

"What do we do?" Hearing footsteps walking upstairs, Hannah took charge (she thought, *why did I wait so long to offer myself as the Lord's servant?*). Taking the priest's hand, she walked them both to her office. She played the message again. "Please!" the boy pleaded, and now this unlikely pair, a humiliated Roman Catholic priest and a now-no-longer backsliding former Baptist, joined soul energies.

Luke said, "We will find this boy and stop this nightmare."

Yet not everyone shared these lofty motives. Later that day Leo expertly pulled the middle school student's chair next to him. "Your parents want you to know all of this and expect me to teach this to you. Let's look at this video together." And the journey into darkness began. The priest reached for his camera. This boy was perfect: so trusting and attentive. "First," he said, "let me position you for some educational videos that will help teach this to other children." He carefully started pushing the boy's clothes around for effect. Not too much today but next week it will come. He took a picture. "You look great! Your parents will be so proud."

After a while, he said, "Let's go take some pictures in the bathroom. There is better light there." The teenager's eyes got big but it sounded reasonable. They walked down to the bathroom. The priest pushed the boy in first and locked the door. He turned on the water as loud as he could. As soon as he had his back to the wall, the priest instructed the boy. "This is how you do it."

Then Leo heard Hannah outside in the hall saying, "Yes, the mice have been running in the hallway and through the bathroom."

Hannah knocked on the bathroom door.

The priest looked at the boy and said, "Next week I'll help you do this. You need to know how. It's part of your education." He unlocked the door and let the boy out.

The exterminator's eyes opened wide when Leo and the acolyte walked out.

Through clenched teeth, Hannah said, "Rats too. We have problems with rats."

But for the rest of the week, the teenager tensed every time he heard running water. He cringed at the memory of being pushed into this room by this priest, and terrified at what could happen to him. What should he do?

Preparing for Latin again, Luke walked into the school. He wanted to scan the faces of the children and see if he could see any signs of distress in a sixth- or seventh-grade boy. *This is hopeless,* he thought. But as he tried to walk by the security nun, Sister Clotilde said with authority, "Father, you know the rules, so bring your briefcase over here. I need to go through everything."

Luke stoically walked over. Doesn't she know that I am a priest and the one who made these rules here? In recognition of his frustration, a waiting mother turned and smiled, saying nothing. Trying to avoid Clotilde's grim authority in her strong stare, he looked over her shoulder. Startled, he inhaled quickly. Clotilde responded quickly, "What's wrong, Father Luke?"

He didn't answer. For in changing his gaze, he saw Leo, his back to Luke, standing outside the door of a classroom looking at cell phone pictures with an older acolyte from St. Charles. Even at a distance he saw the pictures of people in awkward postures. "Oh my God," Luke breathed out, and he knew he was not swearing but begging the divine for help.

Chapter Five

What happens when a priest falls? The abyss reaches out, grabbing and stealing, and the priest loses all light. And tragically, falling right behind the priest are the innocent ones denuded of their protection. Falling into the abyss, strangled by increasing darkness, the void silences their screams.

The diocese of Washington, DC enjoyed the two rivers, Anacostia and Potomac, that twined and surrounded the powerful city. Now in the late afternoon sun, the priest took off his shoes and ran his toes through the sand along the small beach at Haines Point, and, with the warm sun caressing his body, he sat down and waited for the pleasures of the evening. This diocese knew how to live! Cruises, parties, events beyond description, and now rituals next to the water. One by one, at planned intervals priests walked over to meet him, none in collar, all carrying knives and carving wood, all only making minimal greetings.

The leader came and sat surrounded by five priests, and taking a piece of rope, he reached out for the youngest of the group and expertly tying his wrist with rope, wrist to wrist.

"Give him wisdom, my sons," the leader ordered.

Obediently, each stated something.

"We are all together and united."

"We will change the world."

"Seek not yourself but our leader will show the way."

"Life is good for our tribe."

"The glory of all creation rests upon us."

After each statement, the priest handed each new member a whittled cross. They pricked open a finger and let warm blood flow onto the crosses. The priest collected them, piling them in the middle of the group.

Then the leaders stood, "We are one with another now!"

And now the final ceremonies of union, different and mysterious every time. Throwing a gasoline-drenched rag on the crosses, he threw a lighted match on it and watched the shrieking, exploding wood torch the black night skies.

On this beautiful spring afternoon, Oscar took his place on the church steps and began his usual Sunday afternoon concert. He sang out, "O, for a thousand tongues to sing, my great Redeemer's praise!"

The relaxing Peter sat close by, his civilian clothes on so as not to be identified, sunglasses sparkling in the light, while Oscar serenaded the passing spectators.

Hannah, working quietly in her office, heard a door open. She froze and tried to appear relaxed as she saw Carlos enter the room. Quickly, she said, "How are you feeling? I heard you had been sick."

"Better," he said, but he still looked tired. "I'm not sleeping well."

"I am catching up and looking for some of my missing back statements. You know these priests aren't very organized."

Walking out, he responded without looking at her, "To say the least."

Enough of this espionage work, she thought, *maybe they were just disorderly and messy.* She saw the open file with all of the pledge information. In her mind she thought of generations of parishioners, running the gamut from poor to wealthy, who had faithfully brought their checks down to St. Charles. For the first time in this long ordeal, this newly consecrated servant Hannah wept. The faithful flock, so trusting and loving, and giving now to what?

In his room, Luke sat faint with fury. What kind of demon would hurt these young children? And what kind of God would let this go on and on? Where are you, God? Are you with us or not? The God of love, he had learned in seminary, is a God who loves justice. Luke urgently cried out, "We are trying to set this right to end this victimization! Where are you?"

And at midnight Jerry toiled away. Wolves can teach us a lot about devotion to a group. We put so much pressure on the individual for fulfillment that we have forgotten dedication to our group. I guess I learned that from my parents who cared for so many children. Be devoted to God who gives us the family and then so many decisions fall into place.

Wolves travel around, keeping distance from each other for most of the time and then occasionally spend time together. The pack itself is sacred—unless leaders become incapable of caring for the pack.

Later Luke also toiled away in the library. When you make a decision, Ignatius, how do you choose the right thing? Ignatius had written this.

> When you make a decision, first think about the ultimate end of your life: the praise of God and the salvation of your soul.[1]

Okay, Luke thought, *meditate on this.* So think about receiving the invitation into heaven; I want to live, so I hear "Welcome, Home!" But Ignatius had not stopped there:

---

1. Ignatius of Loyola, *Spiritual Exercises*, 164.

> Imagine someone standing in front of you with this same
> situation. What would you tell him to do?[2]

Luke imagined the aging Pope Francis with his funny little squint and the smile ready to break out, standing in front of him, telling Luke about this dilemma.

The pope began speaking. "Father Luke, first I saw pornographic pictures on the church computer. Then I saw suspicious activity between a diocesan official and a child."

Then in his imagination, Luke exclaimed, "No, don't tell me this!" and then slowly, the imaginary pope began to disappear, first the feet and then the head, and with all remaining were the torso, Francis's long index finger shaking accusingly at Luke.

Then Ignatius's words moved closer to Luke's soul as if to whisper his counsel.

> Think about this situation in terms of your inevitable
> death. What do you want to say that you have done?[3]

Luke thought, *I am taken to Georgetown University Hospital so near this church, close to the elegant French Embassy, parks and grassy, rolling fields surrounding the prestigious hospital. What if I were dying on the fifth floor of the GU hospital in the intensive care unit, a circular-shaped unit without windows, only flimsy curtains between the many seriously ill patients, machines beeping, red-eyed relatives walking in, muted conversations with white-jacketed doctors. Beep-beep, alarm sirens, a disjointed music of a cacophony of sounds announcing the ups-and-downs of diseases killing human lives.* How would he think about this church situation when he was leaving Planet Earth? Suddenly Luke found himself as alarmed as the expensive medical machines. Of course he would want to say that if there were even one victim out there he could have helped, he would have offered his assistance.

He imagined another succeeding and even more dismal situation: near Stanton Park in northeast Washington DC in a small dark-brown wood paneled room at the funeral home, sympathetic

---

2. Ignatius of Loyola, *Spiritual Exercises*, 164.

3. Ignatius of Loyola, *Spiritual Exercises*, 165.

black-suited employees with the ready offer of Kleenex and an elegant, decay-proof coffin. And then Luke saw his corpse lying there all alone yet decked out in every vestment known, red, purple, and black and a huge silver crucifix resting on his still chest, with committed Catholics coming in to pay brief respects before their evening drink.

"Such a good Father! So faithful!" they murmured to each other, but no tears of friends and relatives, no sobbing children. Peter came in to lead a short prayer service, with Annette behind him in attendance carrying her silver-beaded evening bag. What would Luke leave behind to show his time upon the earth? What legacy?

And then Ignatius gave him the one-two punch.

Imagine this decision in light of the Eternal Judgment.[4]

Eternal judgment, where human beings are divided away from God or drawn closer to God forever. Would God care about social reputations? That would make God quite superficial. Or wouldn't God care if corrupted priests offered counsel to struggling human beings based on their own sick way of perceiving reality? No question about that. Luke stood up with no lingering indecision. And in his heart, he wondered again, how did you learn so much, Ignatius?

That night Father Luke dreamed over and over about the mass. He was taking his hands and said, "This is my body, this is my blood." He repeated this over and over and under his hands, he saw the real body and blood emerge, with shocking realism. The dying body of a young man appeared with his blood bringing life and his body carrying the divine Spirit. But then Luke stepped back from the altar and saw that now was the time of his own sacrificial work, and that he had prepared for this moment his entire ordained life.

Yet how could he, a middle-aged priest alienated from the church hierarchy and now outraged about crimes against children,

4. Ignatius of Loyola, *Spiritual Exercises*, 165.

do anything? Yet through his mind floated the thought: *who else would do it?* Only someone for whom this is an impossibility.

Immediately upon waking, Luke jumped up, still thinking of eternal damnation, felt a new conviction and added this to his notebook as three.

4. Better to face all we can in this life rather than face punishment in the next.

Another Wednesday: more of the same therapy. Giving Jerry a lift, Luke turned onto Massachusetts Avenue when police with piercing sirens and flashing red lights blocked all the traffic by parking across the lanes. The police cars first, then five black Suburban SUVs with sharpshooters inside and the quickly-flashing limousine. The vice president was coming home to his mansion on the naval observatory and all traffic stopped.

Luke sighed—late for the meeting but when politicians traveled across Washington DC, everything stopped. He drummed his fingers on the steering wheel.

Pressing his lips together, Jerry said, "More rumors, Luke. The bishop . . ." And his shaking voice turned into coughing.

"Let me try again. Wolves have the alpha male; we priests have the bishop. I have heard secretly from Bruce that the bishop has taken several lovers from our priests."

Luke stared at him

"I do not know if it is true, but we need to watch."

The odd man in front of the Vatican embassy now carried a new sign reading, "Catholic Hypocrites." Seeing Jerry hop out of the car, the gray-haired man wandered over to speak to Luke through the window.

"Any news from the abyss?"

Luke turned his head. "There's hope now. I am not listening to this bishop anymore."

"A new word: Look for the criminals!"

Luke felt the hair on his neck stand on end and finally deciding to thank him, looked up to see his window empty and no one standing there. And then the vice president flashed by and Luke gunned it for the meeting.

Hudson was talking. "About priest support, I think it is a choice. The diocese has given us this support group, so in the end it is up to us. We have a choice to do that."

Bruce argued back, "Priests are divided between those who are in or out, and everybody knows which they are."

Hudson added, "I don't experience isolation in my own life. It's telephone and email, and making a commitment to get together in a priest support group. I don't feel that sense of isolation. There is a sense of work and business, and then ten o'clock at night phone calls and get-togethers."

Luke spoke quietly, "What are we even talking about?" A slight pause and then they continued.

Jerry added, "I feel like if I take care of my responsibilities than I am doing a good job."

Then Bruce began the interrogation. "Okay, Jerry. Finish your story about what is going on at St. Charles."

Obediently Jerry started, "I'll tell you what I know. Our adolescent acolyte we talked about last time had found a small room under the sanctuary—a place where pipes and other construction materials were hidden. A week ago a young boy was missing and the grandmother looked everywhere for him. Finally they heard sounds of crying and found the acolyte and the young child in this room."

"So what happened?"

"The acolyte denied anything happened but when asked about the room, said that he had been taken there as a young boy by a priest. No one knows what to believe. We are still waiting to see if the grandmother of the boy sues or not."

"What priest?"

"Nobody knows. Bishop Cahill is supposed to be investigating." Jerry looked down at his lap. "I wish I had a more definitive answer myself. This is church life at its worst and I hate this. This is the second time."

Sighs were heard from around the silent room. Soon they disbanded.

Luke arrived back at the stately wolf statue, walking past relaxed dog walkers. Peter walked around with his watering can, and Oscar was singing, "For the beauty of the earth!" Peter turned around at times and motioned to Oscar who quickly moved in to help his friend pull a weed or a broken flower.

Oscar's voice floated over the pacific church garden, "For the glory of the skies!"

Now was Luke's chance to have a private conversation: he quickened his pace and headed in to talk to Hannah.

Luke told Hannah what had been said about the acolyte at St. Charles.

"Is that the tall one with a large smile?"

"I think so."

"Why is he allowed here?"

"I think some adult here has an attraction to him. Kindred spirits, you know."

"Who's doing this?"

Luke frowned. "Leo must be doing the computer stuff. But is he doing anything with the kids? And is Peter only involved with Annette, or is he involved with the computers and others?"

Hannah stared. "Not sure. We need to do something."

"Okay, Hannah. But in all honesty, we might lose here."

Then out of curiosity, she asked, "What do you priests talk about in your group?"

And Luke, to his surprise, said, "Loneliness." He said quietly, "Okay, I know this won't make a lot of sense to you, my Protestant friend, but I have turned to Ignatius to understand this situation."

She looked blank. "What are you talking about?"

"The founder of the Jesuit order, Ignatius, living in the 1500s in Spain. While recovering from a war injury, he struggled with two ways of thinking: that of the world and that of God, and he developed spiritual exercises to help discern the way to go and which spirits were present: those from the devil or those from God." Luke added, "Get our disordered hearts, minds, and souls ordered before God."

To his surprise, Hannah murmured, "Now I believe in that. My Baptist preacher growing up used to say all the time, choose between God and the devil. I didn't know that you even believed in the devil."

Luke grew pale. "I didn't believe very much until recently. We are up against superior forces and we need deliverance. We don't have a chance here, Hannah."

"Touché," came her quiet response.

Luke said, "All I know is you do the right thing. You do it again. You say your words and stand your ground." Timidly, Luke said, "Talk to you tomorrow, Hannah?"

Her quiet affirmation brightened his spirits.

Chapter Six

What happens when a priest falls? The material body, taunting and victorious, holds the dying soul prisoner and with every final breath, goodness disappears.

Sighing, General Amos Knight stared at his calendar. Every Lent he and his wife gave a dinner party for the St. Charles leaders in their Capitol Hill mansion. At first, these happy dinners brought satisfaction, but now this hung on him like a heavy weight. He had started as a young Air Force officer and believed in the mission of the church as fervently as he did his military operations. Now, though, St. Charles seemed different to him, maybe like a pleasure-seeking social club. No matter, a duty was a duty and he would continue this tradition.

He picked up the phone, "Love," he said gently, "I know you won't like to hear this and I don't want to say it, but the church dinner party is coming up."

She made an irritated noise. "OK. I'll get the caterer lined up for Saturday, March 14, and get the invitations out. Anything else you can think of?"

He smiled at her affection: her duty-filled efficient military wife's soul had kicked into action. They had made it so far together. He had joined the military at a time when African Americans still had a difficult time proving themselves. Yet no one had been able to stop them, working as a team.

Now Jerry stayed up at night to write about his favorite subject. Wolves lived in packs, yet they had tremendous power. They lived life as nomads about half of the year, traveling through harsh winter conditions, making temporary homes in the snow and cold. Yet through their howling at night they encountered one another. At night, they began the beautiful howling with its different sounds pitched from high to low, short guttural barks and melodies as sublime as an opera singer. They knew where each member of the pack was through howling. A wolf could be on a mountaintop, bathed in the colorful Northern Lights, and by howling know where children, parents, and friends were. The nose pointed up, the vocal cords fully engaged, and the sounds, all said: "Where are you? Are you okay? Do you need food? And isn't life beautiful?"

Jerry arose: could the wolf-like quality of communication appear here?

Oscar's nighttime ritual was to sit down next to the wolf statue and croon the spiritual, "What wondrous love is this, O my soul, O my soul, What wondrous love it this?" He put his arm tenderly around the mother wolf statue and leaned his tired head against her back and, sighing, let all his yearning out, singing, "Wondrous love!"[1]

In the blazing orange-reds of the sun setting over the Potomac River, Peter and Jerry headed out to the formal dinner. Peter stared at Oscar and then, turning to Jerry, said, "How I wish I knew his story! Did he have a mother? What happened to him?"

To which the elegant Jerry simply answered, "What happened to all of us? Where is our wondrous love, Monsignor?" And

---

1. Lionel Bart, "Where is Love?" 1960.

with this, the questions ended and off they marched to the dress performance.

The leaders of St. Charles descended for their annual event in the General Knight Capitol Hill mansion: historical brick-red Victorian mansion, two stories with a full basement, a small backyard, and even smaller postage-stamp tiny front yard filled with a white dogwood tree.

Over the salad, the general began his push. Looking directly at the monsignor, "What are your priorities as a leader in the Roman Catholic Church?"

Peter wiped his mouth. "My ministry to the homeless and a youth confirmation class led by Father Leo from the Vatican."

Amos sighed. "I mean our faith; how are we progressing the cause of our church?"

Peter sat impassive while Jerry jumped in the fray, saying, "The bishops have the priests all meeting regularly to build community among us in hopes that we can in turn build community more effectively in the parish." Peter turned and allowed himself a discreet scowl at Jerry.

But the general smelled blood and leaned forward. "Is it working? What do you talk about in your priests' group?"

Unabated, Jerry continued in his loquacious mode, "Personal issues and how to hold our shrinking Catholic numbers of priests together. Sometimes we discuss what kind of leadership we need in the postmodern age."

The general nodded, interested. At least some of the bishops understood the problems our church faces. "With our polarized society, we need these conversations."

Peter now turned to Jerry and allowed himself an amazed look; Jerry's truthfulness seemed to have pleased this important leader.

Then the general actually smiled and with a slight emphasis on the second-person pronoun asked, "What do *you* talk about, Father Jerry?"

And Jerry leaned his head back and laughed, while Peter raised his eyebrows at him, while thinking what else can I do but kick him under the table?

"That is a great question, General. I am beginning to talk more about the glories of our church in the context of the Roman Empire. You know the symbol for Rome was the nurturing she-wolf, and I am writing more and more about that for my PhD dissertation. The Romans understood the power of the symbol of the protecting, ferocious wolf mother and became great through pondering her as a model."

The general felt an inner surge of relief: someone was doing something about this cultural deluge of despair. He turned to the monsignor and said, "It sounds like a good project. If you want, I will head the stewardship campaign this year."

Peter choked on his bread and sputtering could say nothing. The smiling Jerry answered for him. "St. Charles needs you, general, and we are honored to accept your help."

And the general's wife pondered, what caterer will we use for that reception?

Peter reached for the phone that night.

"Leo, what is going on with Jerry? He talked nonstop at the dinner tonight. No sense of control or propriety left in him."

Leo waited.

Peter sighed. "Does he know, Leo? Who knows?"

Leo tried for the comforting remark.

"Knows what, Padre? There is nothing to know. Anyone can get sick."

"It was my one chance to prove myself and I failed at it. Others pull it off."

Peter tried to speak again but Leo stopped him.

"Nothing more, Father. Trust me."

"But Luke knows something. I overheard him talking . . ."

Peter heard the unexpected click of a disconnected phone.

In his small room, Luke reached for his copy of the *Spiritual Exercises*. The warrior Ignatius got it. Wisdom only comes in real danger. Flying into enemy territory, the pilot needs to know the spirit and motivation of his own heart. Then know your enemies' heart, and you have the source of all power. Do this, seek survival, and the blood that is shed will not be your own. To hold the seat of inner power, imagine yourself in a situation and listen to your thoughts rising up.

Luke repeated it out loud: "Wisdom only comes in real danger."

Reading the section the "Greater Discernment of Spirits," he read that Satan aims his weapons at the target of the life of grace to kill the spiritual sense of relationship to God. This enemy of human nature attacks to disturb the soul by suggesting ideas of sick, sensual pleasures. As these corrupting ideas grow stronger, they become substantial vices. Then after accepting the entry of these spirits, the person loses God and all wisdom.[2]

Luke emphasized to himself, *Know and watch for these temptations. Satan plans our destruction. Our conscience biting at us like a dog hopes to save us. In discernment, the good Angel touches the soul sweetly with a drop of water that enters into a dry and rigid sponge. The sponge relaxes and assumes whatever shape the divine ordains for serving our Lord.*[3]

Luke thought, *Ignatius knew how to be alone without being lonely.*

2. Ignatius of Loyola, *Spiritual Exercises*, 205–6.

3. Ignatius of Loyola, *Spiritual Exercises*, 207.

Chapter Seven

What happens when a priest falls? Sorrow, only sorrow.

L uke thought, *In years past when I needed help, I would have turned to a good nun; you know the kind, the one who has looked evil in the face and rapped its knuckles with a firm ruler.* The sounds of running school kids from St. Charles school underneath his window brought back memories of his own education. At seven, he had prayed on his knees while feeling such joy in Jesus. At thirteen he began looking at girls, yet the mystery of Christ beckoned and now in his forties, he had become an aging priest with full years of service behind him.

The next morning Luke faced again the strenuous Sister Clotilde.

"Let me see the backpack," she ordered to an out-of-breath mom.

Then she directed her energies at him, "Father, are you teaching a class this morning?"

Even the demons must avoid this woman, Father Luke reflected. *What she says is, show me your good intentions and I will let you pass. Yet now in our church hierarchy, it is show me you will shut up and accept anything, and I will promote you.*

He remembered his studies in Rome: the red-doffed Swiss guards and the services in St. Peter's Cathedral, so exquisite that the doors in heaven should have swung open right then and there. In his prayers ascending to God in waves of gracious glory while kneeling at the altar, he knew something so grand it broke his heart open.

Luke had talked to a favorite professor, Dr. Sanchez. "Tell me about the soul, David."

He answered quickly, "A part of God that exists before us and placed in us at conception. The soul yearns for union with God and throughout the actions of our lives we will find or will thwart this union. Our soul yearns for freedom of movement and thought, as Ignatius said. Yet in this world, the body, the part that inevitably desires for food, shelter, and sex, pushes the soul around. The soul emerges at times and yearns for integrity and wholeness, truth and love. How do we release our soul from this prison of the body?"

Running her errands, Mrs. Knight stopped by the parish office.

"We are planning for the stewardship reception," she said to Hannah. Then she leaned forward and spoke close to Hannah's ear, "Father Peter is distracted. Can you get his attention? He just goes through the motions."

Frankly, Hannah responded, "I saw him sitting at his desk late on Sunday evening. He didn't even seem to know I was here. "

The general's wife backed off. "The next time Peter seems alert, please ask him a date for the reception."

Then Hannah's decision became clear. Later she called Luke in his room. "We don't know enough about what is on that computer. My nephew Eric works in computer forensics. I am calling him tonight."

Without a word, Luke and Hannah agreed to this plan and separated; or had they? For spirit had joined to spirit, soul to soul, and the two shall become one.

That evening on her cell phone, "Aunt Hannah, what in the world are you talking about? Could you slow down a bit," Eric requested. His mind, so used to detailed and careful analysis, could not understand this new Aunt Hannah who seemed to be infected by the Bible. What had she just quoted to him from the prophet

Amos, "Let judgment flow down like the waters"? Judgment or justice? Jehovah? Or does it matter: she wanted some "J" word to flow down on this church. And when did Hannah start reading the Bible? Eric took a bite of his apple and waited.

In response to the confused Eric, Hannah, the recently consecrated servant of the living Lord, smiled. *I guess this is puzzling to everyone,* she thought. Carefully she explained. "Something very dreadful is going on at my work at St. Charles. I saw a priest and an acolyte in the bathroom together and some other boy keeps calling the church message system and asking for help. I looked at the priests' computer with its pornography and an odd picture of a teenage boy's blurry face sprang up."

Eric froze. "Are you sure, Hannah?" He forgot the reverential title of Aunt he always used to remind him of her sweet presence throughout his childhood.

"I will never forget the horror of this, Eric. I am sure."

Eric rubbed the back of his neck. "And you want me to . . . ?" Then anger shot through him. "The people who make it should be . . ."

Hannah interrupted. "You got it. We need to get the evidence off of the computer and see what is going on. Don't you know how to do that?"

"Of course. I do that all the time."

"Tonight then, darling? All the other priests are gone now for a retreat."

Eric sighed. *Some porn has the mob written all over it.* Yet Hannah was reverting to quotes from the prophet Amos and he didn't even want to start touching that subject again.

"Tonight at midnight."

"Meet you in front of the church. Oh, and I am bringing the one priest I trust; actually he's now banned from Sunday mornings at the church. What better recommendation is there? His name is Luke."

And call me Ishmael, Eric muttered to himself. *My aunt quotes prophets, she has a friend who can't keep a job, and now I am in the middle of a midnight tryst at a gloomy church. I hope* this never makes my resume. Jumping Jehoshaphat, I hope judgment, justice, and Jehovah protect us with this one.

That night the cold wind whipped around and the bare trees swayed in a powerful wind. The flagpoles clanged as their chains hit, announcing bizarre news, and even the church looked as if it might break apart under the power of the dark night.

Walking in the front gate, the tall, blonde Eric saw his sweet Aunt Hannah next to Father Luke, both standing as if frozen. Eric's backpack full of equipment clanged against his body. Usually he made images of computer hard drives for already established legal investigations and received the handsome pay of about $20,000 a report. No one blamed him for anything: he only came in after the war between two clients began. He always wondered why people weren't more careful about what they put on their computers. Didn't they know that anything you download or write could never be successfully deleted? The hard-drive of a computer is like a permanent tablet taken directly from Mount Sinai, but the widespread ignorance about this had given him an excellent career.

Eric looked straight ahead. He had brought the tools of a postmodern knight on his stallion to help. Seeing Luke's eyes full of questions, Eric explained, "The tools I use are standard forensic tools and are often used by law enforcement, spy agencies, and in civil litigation for electronic discovery. The first one creates an image of the hard drive." Seeing Luke's unresponsive face, Eric paused. "I can find anything—emails, browsing history, and deleted files." He waited for questions but none came. "I do this mainly for courts, never my relatives."

They unlocked the parish office door furtively and walked into the shared priests' office. Several computers greeted his sight. Hannah pointed to the one against the back wall as she logged into the computer. Her access to the computer allowed this legal entry. She then invited Eric to look at the computer. He walked over and expertly going into the control panel, found the browser history.

"Good Lord in heaven," came out of his mouth. A whole range of titles popped out like demons from hell.

Hot and sexy.

X-rated.

And then—"Little Sluts."

"Never too young."

Eric turned to see Hannah and Luke huddled together, looking like cattle trying to find some warmth in a raging storm. "Come over and see this."

They drew near and then the quiet of heaven descended on them. Did God want them to see this? What evil had visited here? What questions needed answering?

Eric frowned. "Most computers aren't as disgusting as this church one."

No time for this. Eric whispered, "Go watch to make sure no one comes in. This will take about two hours. I will copy the hard drive and then analyze it for you in the next few days."

Eric took out his small machine, plugged it in, and began the work of uncovering that which is hidden.

Most of the long night, Eric toiled away copying the St. Charles church computer.

The next day, Eric got up and sleepily rolled over. Was that a nightmare about seeing all that pornography on the St. Charles church computer? No: the perplexed looks on Hannah and Luke's faces were engraved on his mind. Suddenly energized, Eric ran for the copied hard drive and his bag. "I'm going to work early today. Let's see what we have here."

The JPEG files kept coming and kept coming. When they reached over a hundred images, Eric stopped and started looking.

Eric sent a quick text. "You are right, Aunt Hannah."

Luke and Hannah grabbed a grilled cheese sandwich at the local Five Guys. Getting the huge order of French fries (made from Idaho potatoes this time) and a plate of unshelled peanuts, words burst out quickly.

Hannah started, "Okay. What do we do? Problems and maybe crimes. We could go to the DC city authorities, but what if they call the diocese to tell them who complained and we are finished?"

Luke slowed down in his shelling peanuts. "I think that is Eric's role to send this to the authorities. Yet even if we go to the police, some of them will be Catholic and possibly too intimidated by their church education to question and challenge a bishop and his diocese."

Hannah said, "So we assume Eric notifies some authority and they don't do anything. That leaves us to help the poor kid who keeps screaming about the running water."

Distantly, Luke noticed the constant traffic climbing up Wisconsin Avenue. "I know what is expected of us next, Hannah. A conversation with Peter."

Hannah stared. "You mean you will tell him about what we know?"

"I think I will start with a conversation about child safety with Peter. Just to see how he reacts and see what clues I get from him about what is happening."

Later that afternoon, Luke saw Peter sitting in his office. Luke began. "Monsignor, can I talk with you for a moment?"

Peter stood up from behind his impressive desk and walked around. He briefly glanced at his cell phone and then placed it on the desk.

"Surely, Luke. I don't have an appointment for another hour."

The image of the adolescent boy had haunted Luke since he saw this.

"I am not sure of the boy's name, but last Sunday I saw a teenage boy going into the childcare room with a cell phone in hand."

Suddenly steely, the monsignor looked at Luke. Sighing, he said, "What are you talking about?"

Suddenly Luke's words forced themselves out in a fashion he had not planned. "Cell phones make movies, don't they? I am afraid of what is going on with the children here. Are they safe? Are we protecting them as a church? I have seen that same boy approaching the kids before. I am afraid that he is taking pictures of them without their parents' permission."

Peter stiffened. "What in the world are you suggesting?"

"Child pornography. I hear it's all over the internet and a very real danger. What are we doing about it? To make sure our children live in security and know who is around them. Have we vetted that boy and trained him? Do you remember our own training, Monsignor, when we saw the movie with child molesters talking about how they did these crimes? They kept saying that they needed other adults who would not confront them to get away with this."

Standing up, Peter stood. "Father, we don't have any problems here. We have large, well-run programs and are financially stable. I don't want to hear you bringing up such odd subjects again." He stood up and walked back to his desk. Luke walked out feeling like a failure: so much for the direct approach. And why did he feel so foolish when he had tried to talk about this?

Back in his room, Luke paced around, thinking about the church computer. He had to take this to Bishop Cahill. Maybe he would be understanding and stop all of this right away.

He dialed the diocese and soon explained to the bishop's secretary. "Yes, I am sure I need to talk to the bishop right away."

"Let me see," was all she promised.

Soon Luke heard Hannah's purposeful voice on his phone.

"A call has come from the diocese, Luke. You are to go to a meeting that is set up next week."

Luke trembled.

Without him saying a word, Hannah ordered, "Now, Father Luke, you will go and speak truth to power. No, I don't know who first said that phrase . . ."

Luke interrupted, "The Quakers said it first."

"Good for them! We are not pretending to be a leaf shaken in the wind or a piece of flotsam driven by the tide. We are now like trees planted by the water. Stand tall, speak truth, and give this to the bishop and maybe he will even do something."

All of these Biblical images asserted themselves in Luke's mind at once, completing the word of Saint Ignatius: believe divine justice accompanies us and maybe at times this very justice appears.

"Yes, Hannah. Thank you."

As Luke stood, something flashed through his mind like a bird taking flight. Even as he resented this situation, he could see some good working in his life. Maybe this was redemption. "I have new friends, I understand some of Ignatius's thought, and I am going to a meeting with the bishop." Maybe, just maybe, he was on his way to being—well, to use Hannah's phrase—born again. For the first time in weeks, Luke laughed.

The huge northwest brick Tudor mansion housed the church offices.

Clutching the disk with the catalog of browser history and the porn sites visited, Luke sat in the elaborate reception room filled with antique furniture waiting for his appointment with Bishop Cahill. Through a cracked-open door, Luke saw the bishop getting some papers out of a file while talking briefly to his administrative assistant.

The bishop's booming voice rang out. "Come in, Father Lucas, how good to see you!"

Luke winced. Did the bishop know that he was called Luke? No time to think now.

Cahill motioned Luke to a chair next to his desk. "I am so glad we have made time to be together. With my busy schedule, this does not happen enough. How are you, Father? How is your ministry going?"

Luke leaned forward, "Unfortunately, Bishop, I have brought some bad news. I discovered that someone is looking at pornography on the St. Charles church computer. I brought a . . ."

The bishop cleared his voice stood up and walked behind his desk. Eyes averted away from Luke, he picked up the papers and came to sit down. "I suppose that this was done by the church janitor. You have one there—isn't his name Pablo or something like that? Unfortunately those from that low-class walk of life frequently do this. We must pray for him and I'll have Leo talk to him about this."

Luke said, "No, I found it on the computer after Monsignor Peter left the room."

Bishop Cahill began, "I care about your career, Lucas. If you start repeating innuendo and gossip, I will be forced to put a warning in your file."

Luke responded, "But this is true! If we don't do something, people's lives will be harmed. I care about that and not anyone's file. The people attending the church could be in danger."

Cahill sighed. "After all the resources the diocese has put into addressing the problems of priestly relations, do you still hate your fellow priests? Of course, your file already has lots of unfortunate comments about your imagination."

All Luke could see was a huge frown on Bishop Cahill's face. "Lucas," he said firmly, "I was going to share with you a report that our good Monsignor filed about you recently. He said you seem restless and uneasy. And now I see the truth of what Father Peter said who also expressed concern about your rational abilities. It seems that your sermons keep talking about faith alone and not about the great intellectual traditions of our beloved Catholic Church. Father Peter also said that you have befriended the church secretary and date her now. We think you need some help. I will send Leo to you soon with some directives about how you can regain your stability and protect any ministry that you have left."

"But, Bishop, I brought you a copy of everything that is on the computer and what time the pornography is being viewed."

Cahill's frown deepened. "You seem deluded, Lucas. Leave it with me. Go rest and soon you will hear from Leo."

Luke knew he should stop but instead, "Leo is a sexually active . . . ."

"Stop, Lucas, or you will force me into actions I do not wish to do." He reached over and made a motion under his desk.

The bishop's secretary suddenly opened the door.

Shaking his head, Luke walked out the door. He turned around with his last missive. "Men, women, and children have rights, Bishop. Pope John XXIII said that. Judgment begins in the household of God. St. Paul said that."

The secretary's words spat out at him. "Leave now."

And Luke turned out and in a blur headed for the diocesan door.

Walking outside, Luke's ears were ringing as he walked right past the odd man carrying his sign reading "Catholic Hypocrites!" Luke turned towards him and declared, "You're right. I don't need this bishop telling me what to do." Giving him thumbs up, Luke left, energized by his unexpected anger.

Later that day, Bishop Cahill called in Leo. "That fool Father Luke reported Peter today for pornography. I told him that we suspected the janitor. Write up a letter of suspension for Luke without stating the reason. Send it to him. This anxiety will push him over the edge. Maybe we can get rid of him that way."

Leo smiled. "Luke was that way even when studying in Rome. We played some game on him one time and he is still upset about it." He paused and looked at Cahill. "We had such a good time in Rome, didn't we, bishop? Dinners, theaters, late nights, and all of those parties. Poor Luke—he just doesn't get it." He thought for a second. "Of course you are absolutely right. Let's suspend him. Maybe he will decide to go to some old priest's home and play shuffleboard all day."

Cahill stopped. "Peter needs our help. When Luke gets this, he will be stampeding out of there."

Two days later, Bishop Cahill and Father Leo walked into the Washington, DC basilica for the annual meeting of the clergy. The immense cathedral with its fancy chapels reached a zenith of beauty with its high sparkling ceiling glittering with golden images of heaven, angels, and heaven everlasting. Now priests converged in the worship space to hear direction from their bishop. Seeing

Peter, Cahill called out, "What a joy to see you! I've taken care of everything." In a softer voice, "This is all part of the adventure of church life, Father."

In front of the assembled priests, Bishop Cahill stood up to give his annual bishop's address. He ended fervently. "You all have to get this right. We are a hierarchical church and you need to make sure that you only say what the diocese informs you to say. The bishops think and you obey, but you have full certainty that in your obedience you will find a reward." After the bishop's address, Cahill enjoyed a standing ovation by the large group of scowling priests. At the first signal from the bishop to sit, everyone sat. Then the bishop grabbed the microphone and looking something like Liberace, said, "Now I want all of my staff to come forward." Some impatient priests sighed, while all hoped that whatever he did would be brief.

About fifteen people wondered forward, mainly female administration assistants and several priests entirely dressed in black with a white clerical collar. Bishop Cahill offered an extemporaneous explanation of what each person did, faltering at what some of the women's actual duties were, though he said things like, "We can't get along without Debbie!" Then Cahill said, "It is time for my annual bishop's award for the greatest contribution this year." Then he announced, "Father Leo, come get your award." He handed him an envelope with an undesignated sum of cash inside. Turning to the still-attentive priests, Cahill continued. "On loan from the Vatican, Leo handles the day-to-day details of the diocese, and any situation I give to him. In his capable hands any problem is dealt with and becomes part of a creative solution." A priest sitting in the front started applause that weakly filled the room.

The bishop continued, "And to honor the occasion, I have composed a poem for Leo." He turned to the captive staff who were looking off in all directions. Then the bishop grabbed the microphone and postured himself in front of the diocesan council. A poem burst forth from his lips with his own original words.

> Give my respect to Leo!
> Remember him on Capitol Hill!

See him in the White House to bring them to our church.
Tell us about his service, and his great sermons to boot,
Give my respect to Father Leo,
May a cardinal's hat be yours!

Cahill's voice audibly cracked at the last word.

Luke felt a pain in his stomach and noticed a green look on the priest sitting to his left. What had he just seen? The older priest next to Luke muttered, "Leo just got ten extra lovers. Or more! Who can say no to him now?"

Luke saw the opening, "What about the bishop? Is he the same?"

"You must be joking. You don't know? Are you the only one not invited?"

"Yes," was Luke's simple answer.

Chapter Eight

What happens when a priest falls? The loss of innocence means the growing and spreading loss of all other gifts. Clinging to nothingness, leering at others, the abyss threatens and draws. Falling, he screams.

As Eric walked to Hannah's apartment, his mind scattered in many directions. What were they up against here? There has to be more information about this somewhere and, remembering a contact named Kevin, he decided he needed a confidential conversation tomorrow.

Three imperfect persons brought together for what? Mutual self-destruction? Or the routing of an evil force established at a church?

Eric, Hannah, and Luke briefly got together at her apartment near American University.

Eric began. "So this is what we have found. On the church priests' computer, there are lots of pornographic images, but none I can identify as children, though some look quite young. Authorities usually look the other way for pornography, but not for child porn. They look for those both making and using child porn."

Luke tried to make a contribution. "All I can tell you is the suspicion about the acolyte taking his cell phone in the childcare area. He might be taking pictures of them and giving them to Leo." He added, "Ignatius would call this spiritual desolation. We are looking at the footprints of demons that need the antidote of direct action."

Hannah responded, "We've got to try to do something or go down trying. Something is wrong with this boy continuing to call the church." Silence. "You know," she added, "The Lord protects his own."

They all broke out laughing. Where was the Lord when all this was set up?

Luke said, "You know, Hannah, you would make a great nun."

Hannah said, "Oh, no. I know now that I am a child of the Protestant Reformation. And I am getting ready to nail my 95 theses on the door of this church and give them a piece of my mind. This is crazy and getting crazier!"

Both Luke and Eric looked somber.

"So where do we stand? What is next?"

Eric said, "I need to find out what law enforcement agency to send this drive to." Looking at his aunt's staring eyes, Eric answered, "That's all I know."

Luke said, "At least you have some good news of some possible action. I took the evidence we have about this computer to Bishop Cahill." Luke's hands folded in his lap. "He refused to look at it or believe me. And he said that I am out of St. Charles and am ordered into therapy." Then he added, "The diocese of Washington deserves better."

Hannah said, "This is really surprising. You would think that he would want to stop this problem and be appreciative of your efforts."

Slowly Luke shook his head in agreement.

Eric said, "OK. Our proactive efforts could do some good but we have no assurance of anything. I propose a spot-checking on the computer every nine or ten days. We also call the police if we see any signs of active involvement with kids. One more thing. Do we have any contacts in Rome?"

For the first time, Luke looked hopeful. "I had a seminary professor who is a canon lawyer in Rome."

Eric spoke softly. "Luke, you need to contact him and report Cahill's aggressive behavior against you, not the others now, but you."

Luke went home, picked up his pen to write the letter to his Vatican professor. "Dear David," he began. Then *what am I doing? The mailed letter will take a week and make me look like I'm left behind in a distant generation.* He went down to Hannah's computer and began googling David Sanchez's name, his current position in Rome with his PhD in Canon Law, and his email.

"Hi, David. Do you remember me?" Rejected as too low key. "Dear Dr. Sanchez. I was in your class." Rejected as too formal. Then "David, I was in seminary with you and now am in trouble and need your help. Bishop Cahill is acting aggressively against his priests." Direct and truthful. Luke composed the rest of this email, pressed send and went up to his room. They had reached out for another source of help. Surely, someone, anyone, would come help.

Later that day Hannah buzzed his room urgently. "Luke," she whispered, "It's your friend from Rome calling. Come quick."

Dr. David Sanchez said only, "Luke, I remember our theological discussions. I will be at Georgetown University next week for a Jesuit conference. " He waited. "As I am sure you understand, the operative word is quiet. Let us come up with a cover story because they will know my name." He added, "I will need proof," and as soon as Luke heard this, he knew what should happen.

Jerry's passion continued. After making a large dinner for some parishioners, he returned to his room. Seeing his desk bathed in moonlight, he walked to his desk. So wolves hunted together and shared their food with each other. *I understand that joy,* Jerry thought. *We work together and then enjoy the goodness of life as we celebrate together.*

Jerry continued thinking. *Wolves understood the change of position in the pack.* When a wolf was the leader, he had to do certain things. He had to watch out for the wellbeing of each member. He had to look at the terrain and know where satisfaction would be found: good food, a warm den, safety for the cubs, stable friendships.

Some wolves lost the ability to lead well. Then a fight happened between two males. Huge and deadly fights with teeth bared, growling, tearing each other apart until rich blood flowed freely, while the other wolves watched from a distance. The winner of this brawl became the leader and the loser became thrown out, alienated, gone forever. The lone wolf then stood without the protection of the pack.

Jerry understood. Life required these fights. When a leader became weak or deranged or both, he placed the entire pack in danger of death.

Late that night, Luke heard quiet footsteps going down into the basement hall, followed by an opening and a shutting noise. There was an underground passage large enough for a grown man to enter that led from the basement hall into a childcare room. This room had been painted a glossy gold and red. It now housed an open space that looked like a shrine to something.

Leo crawled in and the thought of what was coming made him smile. Maybe we can film here and put some shadowy pictures out into cyberspace. The very thought of this made him feel creative and adventurous. Who knew that ordination could lead into such unusual endeavors? He arranged the cameras, put out some aged brandy and snifters. The stage was set for the party.

What a foolproof plan! I'll start letting Cahill know what we will do. Maybe this will inspire him to start arranging my next promotion.

Leo cleaned up further, and planned what exploits they would engage in. Maybe even the bishop will want to be filmed. *You know, the group at the Vatican they worked through thought it very edgy and interesting with their location in this established church from Washington, DC,* Leo reminded himself. *Let them know it is coming. They will send us a handsome check to cover our expenses.* Though he knew that Cahill would gladly pay for this himself without regard to the cost.

Leo remembered the priest from Italy who had made all of this possible. He had told Leo that the brothers would help him and he should join. At first their parties in Rome shocked him and he walked home late at night in shame. But in time he understood that this was a perk of the church game. Now he wanted to introduce everyone to it.

The next Monday, Cahill looked through the list of priests in the diocese. As he looked through, he realized that he had overlooked one of them: Father Jerry, that young, good-looking man who worked for Peter. "I need to get him in for a meeting."

As the tall Leo walked in to share the latest gossip, Cahill asked him, "What do you know about Jerry?"

Leo smiled. "I've never seen him at any of our parties."

Cahill paused. The newest conquest had begun. "Let's invite him next week and have some fun."

"You are fabulous, Bishop. It's done."

The next day an envelope arrived at St. Charles. Standing in the office, Jerry muttered to Luke, "An invitation has come for me." Jerry groaned. "An invitation to one of the Saturday night parties. How do these priests do this on Saturday and then preach on Sunday?"

But he knew how they did it: absolute company men believing in the power of absolution. Nothing they did stuck to them, they thought. Get absolution and move on to the next victim. He had heard rumors about these secret parties and did not want to be involved.

Luke ordered, "Don't turn this down yet. Wait until you hear from me."

Then running to the email, Luke wrote carefully,

> Dear David,
> While at Georgetown University, would you like to attend a bishop's party anonymously with another priest from St. Charles?
> Luke

The terse email flew back from Italy saying only,

> Yes. Don't give my name to anyone, not even the person who accompanies me.

And Luke, remembering some war movie, responded to the communication.

> Roger Wilco.

Jerry sat in his room, wrestling with his dilemma. Did he fall into the trap of going to the party because the bishop controlled so much of his career, or did he show moral courage and reject this invitation and suffer the consequences? Then he heard a small knock on his door. He opened it a crack and saw Luke standing there with a white bag in his hand. What in the world has happened to Luke? He smiles and frowns now; he formerly used to look impassive all the time.

Jerry opened up, saying formally, "Luke, I'm glad you've come. What can I do for you?"

Luke said loudly, "I have brought Krispy Kreme doughnuts."

"Excuse me, what did you say?"

Luke held up his white bag. "Krispy Kreme," he said firmly. "The best doughnuts in the world. My nieces and nephews eat them all the time."

Jerry looked carefully and then started smiling. He didn't even know Luke had a family. "Okay. Come in!"

Luke took out their treat and gave some to the younger priest. Wiping the sugary frosting off his face, Luke said quietly, "I have a favor to ask. I can't tell you much about this, but you need to accept the invitation to the bishop's party. I am sending someone with you."

"Who?" Jerry immediately responded.

"I can't tell you. I am beginning to notice this diocesan dance. This is what you should do. I have a good friend who will go to the party with you. If the bishop and Leo show any surprise, just say he is your family's priest who unexpectedly came into town from San Francisco. Stick to this friend like your life depended upon it. Actually, it might."

Jerry stopped, "And what else?'

"That's all."

"You want me to go to a party with a person I do not even know and pass him off as my family priest?"

"Yes."

"This is nuts."

"My friend says you cannot know anything else."

Jerry stared at Luke's now vibrant eyes and asked, "Should I let Hannah know to RSVP?"

"I already have. On Saturday come to my room at 8 p.m. and I'll introduce you."

Saturday evening was beginning to look pretty interesting.

The next day, Luke slipped in late to their group therapy. He heard Bruce whine, "Terrible daily schedule!"

Luke's fingers slowly drummed on the arm of the chair. Hadn't he heard all of this before?

Dr. Wagner began formally this day. "What makes a good bishop? And how do we support a bishop placed over us?"

Hudson spoke solemnly, "I would like to know if the new bishop is a careerist or if he actually cares about the church. He has to be loyal to us and the people. If it is just his career, the church suffers."

Bruce offered, "He has no concept of the workload. He needs to know how much we do. Then I'll support him."

Jerry spoke out. "I would hope that the bishops would pose the good questions about our lives. We are lonely. I would like to see the leadership address those kinds of issues rather than say we don't have enough priests or the workload is getting heavier and heavier and we don't know where we are going." Jerry looked down and said softly, "Even wolves suffer when they are the lone one."

Wagner probed, "How can we help?"

No answer came from anyone.

Wagner tried again. "Have the bishops been different in their approaches?"

Bruce took that one on. "Yo-yos. That is the understatement. Right wing, left wing, no wing." Laughter met his apt statement.

Jerry took a chance. "A little group in this diocese makes all the decisions. Then they come and try to convince us that we are all part of the conversation."

Luke interjected, "I think we are all certainly frustrated with our work. Jerry is right. We are just holding on like lone wolves."

Jerry built on this. "A lone wolf is the one looking for his family and tribe, those to whom he will commit his life in loyalty. We need the group for whom we sacrifice. Maybe if we see that we need this group, some of our frustration will leave."

Hudson pondered. "Interesting. I think we need to take into account what has happened, particularly in the last few months after rumors about a priest soliciting men in a park. Emotional. You have to see that as part of the picture here. Our whole group's reputation has suffered. How supported does the bishop feel? Does he feel let down?"

Wagner nodded his head up and down. "This surely needs to be discussed. Next time, fellows?"

No one met the others' eyes as the priests filed out of the room.

Early next morning, Annette went to wake up Andrew for school with her usual soft voice.

"Time to get up, honey."

No answer.

More firmly, "Andrew, it is time for school."

In previous years, he would have sat up with a cheery, "Hi, Mom!" But now after a long pause, he only grunted in answer. Her husband Ben came to take him to school and Andrew left without having uttered one word and later she found his uneaten breakfast on the table.

Sitting with another cup of coffee, she worried about his change. Did she have a part in this? She would go talk to Peter about this today.

Seeing Annette dressed in black leggings, red shirt, and catchy gold scarf walking toward the quiet rectory, Luke sighed. *This makes all of us feel bad,* he thought as he recognized the troubled mother's dilemma. From Saint Ignatius, Luke knew the methods of Lucifer. Luke could almost hear Annette's inner thoughts.

First she has a shiny attractive idea: have a drink; watch a movie; spill out the contents of one's heart too quickly to the authoritative priest. Like a golden beautiful veil of light, the attractive idea feels good. "A slight fling with the priest won't hurt anyone. And what fun! Drop the kids by school and go by the priests' office and have some "me time." Isn't that why we go to church: to get a little relief from our problems?"

Soon the spiritual veil of sparkly beauty becomes a little too tight.

"Why does he pay so much attention to my son? What if he tells my husband about our caresses?"

The mother justifies, "The diocese must be vetting and watching these church leaders."

And then the noose tightens. "I saw a priest pat my son too tenderly."

Then in the twinkling of an eye, the Day of the Lord arrives and it is a day of gloom and darkness.

Annette cried, "My God, what have I done? My son has changed and I don't know what has happened. Yet I might be exposed if I report him."

And the beautiful golden veil, as shiny as the sun, has become a strangling rope hanging one's self until death, tying one down and all one can see is the shame and degradation painted on one's own children. And now sin is visited to the second and third generation.

Intimacy, it's all about intimacy. Yet sharing the secrets of one's heart in the context of sin triples the danger. The angel of light brought the tidings of easy pleasure and soon life morphed into a living horror. For these imprisoned souls tied up and entrapped in a mortal torment, darkness has its way.

After another confirmation class, Leo spoke in a confidential tone to Andrew, "Do you have any friends that would like to go to the next Nationals game? They don't have to come to church. This will be our outreach project."

Chapter Nine

What happens when a priest falls? The surrounding group feels the attacking wind ripping through the open door and wonder, who is falling next? And the falling one can only see the haunted faces of those he destroyed. Dread becomes his food and drink.

That night Luke heard a falling sound, like a full laundry bag being tossed down the stairs. I've got to go see. He looked out the window and saw nothing but heard the clear sound of echoing footsteps walking into the sanctuary building. For a brief instant, Luke saw an alternative path for him: that of crawling back into bed, and making up a story, that this was the janitor Carlos making sure that the pipes weren't dripping. His urgency, though, drove him into the green garden, alive with chirping crickets and cicadas.

Luke could hear nothing more over the sound of the insects. Had they gotten away? Then he heard a door softly opening into the church basement. Luke clung to the side of the dark buildings so no shadow would be cast, heading toward the same door. Down one side of the building, over to the other and clinging to the last wall, he found the door and softly crept down the old rickety stairs.

Luke saw that directly under the sanctuary, this small basement room was lighted up with spotlights. The seminarian was running quickly up the stairs and headed out the door. Stunned, Luke began to shake and ran after him. "Wait, wait!" he cried as loudly as he dared through his panting voice. "I want to help!" But the young man, moving at the speed of panic, ran off into the covering darkness.

Luke walked to his Wednesday afternoon ritual, the cleansing-the-air and trying-to-make-a-run-for-bishop group. Let these amazing conversations begin: moments of unbelievable honesty and totally concealed ambition. And it's darn difficult to tell the difference.

Yet as soon as Luke walked in, he knew this was no "business as usual" group. As Luke walked in he heard, "There is another person running the diocese with the bishop right now." Never one to understand group dynamics, Luke looked around to see if signs of recognition identified these two powerful players. Yet even he knew that was Cahill and Leo.

Bruce began, "Dr. Wagner, I want to speak openly."

"Don't you always?" the therapist responded, with his suggestion greeted by smiles.

"The diocese is looking for a priest and the questioning is getting on my nerves."

Hudson sat up straighter.

"Rumors are still flying about the priest soliciting sex. We all feel tainted by this crummy story."

Wagner quickly responded. "Who is the priest? Does anyone know?"

"I don't know but the rumors seem to circle St. Charles again. Once they find him, he'll be finished. The rumors have gone too far to hide."

"It's like what happened in Columbus, Ohio," he heard one priest mutter, and the priests spontaneously began to talk at the same time.

Speaking in a loud voice, Dr. Wagner said solemnly, "Our time today is almost up and I need to talk with you about something important. My wife's baby is due in a week, and I am taking time off for paternity leave."

Luke nodded, while he felt like jumping up in delight.

"I told the bishops that you all are a thoughtful group and would do fine supporting each other for the few weeks I am gone."

The group nodded in unison.

"If I turn this group over to someone else, I might not get it back. And I have become attached to you and want to continue here."

Jerry found his voice first. "And thank you, doctor, for your confidence in us. We hope we do not disappoint you." Wagner's eyes glistened with a soft glow, while the priests all murmured words of support for his leave.

Luke exploded in laughter as they walked down Massachusetts Avenue. "Don't disappoint you, Dr. Wagner! And the first thing we are going to do is drop this official lingo and tell me what you think of these brother priests."

Laughing, Jerry joined in the merriment. "Well, Bruce—spiritual and impetuous. He seems constantly on the verge of leaving the priesthood yet actually is quite committed."

Jerry paused. "The one to watch is Hudson. He is up for promotion, but I sense something here that bears watching."

Instantly the mood changed and Luke remembered ghostly, imploring hands reaching out to him. The rest of their walk back was enveloped in quiet.

Luke returned to the rectory in time to see a brilliant shooting star, the color of the green prairie grass from his beloved Kansas heritage. Wow, the beauty of creation! Or was it more? Could God also be celebrating?

The next week therapy group met for the first time without the trained leader. Jerry began, "Wagner's gone so it is up to us now."

Bruce guessed, "Look at the situation in the diocese: priests being promoted without public signs of excellence while others disappear without signs of problems. It's like a game of Chutes and Ladders without any rational or spiritual basis."

He started laughing, "And you, Luke, are the next disappearing priest. Are you going home to Kansas?"

Luke joined in, "Only if a tornado comes and claims me!"

Jerry walked through the opening, "The point being, Cahill is up to some peculiar work here."

Reluctantly, Hudson entered in, "Rumors, only rumors though, of some secret brotherhood going on in our already secret society."

The FBI selected its agents for the child exploitation unit from those not of a sensitive nature. Looking at the pictures will eat you alive.

"Are you sure you want this assignment?" the official asked Dan. "It requires looking for hours at images that will haunt you day and night."

Dan spoke with conviction, "I want to do this assignment for the protection of children."

Dan remembered the sweet kiss of his five-year-old Melora last night. "Do you remember," she said, "when you washed me in the sink?" She giggled. "I was so little."

"I remember," he said.

Melora smiled. "You got soap in my eyes sometimes."

Dan made only a slightly fake grimace. "I am so sorry!"

Then running to him, she grabbed him. "I love you always. If you get scared, you come and tell me. Or if you have a bad dream, you come and tell me."

Dan looked at Melora and ruffled her hair. But even now, something another agent told him popped into his mind: lots of the time, child molesters start off by rubbing the hair.

How could he accept a position like this? Would his mind be forever poisoned? But as Melora ran to bed in her footy pajamas, he thought, if my work stops one child from being molested, I'll do it. Yet, with her mother gone now, how will I stand the pressure of this work?

Exhilarated, Luke walked quickly back to the church. Yet as he approached, he slowed down some. This work always began with a sense of dread: what was he doing moving into spiritual places without any control? Yet as he thought of not engaging with this, he thought of the boy's terrified voice, "Help me! The water is running."

Into a spiritual place then, he would travel. He took out his small pocket notebook.

Signs that Attracted my Attention

5. God feels like warm fire yet when I enter this church I feel desolate.

6. God puts up with a lot of awful things but God seems to ask me to do something.

No dread now, Luke prayed. We need an interpretation to understand what to do next. How do we protect these children?

The next morning Luke greeted the student with his algebra book sitting open before him in study hall. "What are you working on?"

"Not much." The freckled middle student looked at him and suddenly countered with, "Do you like to work?"

Luke thought of all the mysteries surrounding this situation that needed understanding and his reluctance to work on them. "Not all times, but sometimes."

The student laughed. "Okay, okay. Let me try again."

Walking into their shared home, Luke heard Peter speaking. "What did you say happened? A priest, drunken and high, approached some men and propositioned them for sex." His flat voice offered no possible interpretation.

Luke, sitting in the other office, sat as quietly as he could so Peter would not know he was here.

Peter continued, "Now the men in the park are repeating the story all over town?"

He cursed.

"No, chancellor, you misunderstood me. I said, shoot, I mean I am so surprised that you need to tell me more."

Then Luke heard Peter slam his fist on the table and muttered in a low, tense voice. "Tell me this is not happening. No! This cannot be true." Silence.

"Of course we will not cooperate with the authorities. Of course not."

Luke did not move until long after he heard Peter's slow steps dragging up the rectory stairs.

Now Luke needed to interpret the signs of God because he knew that his very survival depended upon this. *I don't need this bishop telling me what to do*, echoed through his mind.

Was that the smell of cigarette smoke? Who smoked around here now?

At his computer consulting firm, Eric almost barked into his phone. "Hey, Kevin, didn't you used to work at the Obscenity and Child Exploitation division at the FBI?"

Kevin sat back. He had never heard this tone of voice from Eric before. "Yes, great place. I retired from there."

"I need to talk to you. Confidentially?"

"Sure."

"I found some porn on a local church computer along with a blurry picture of what looks like a teenager. I copied the hard drive but don't know what to do next."

"Wow. Pretty rough stuff but the numbers of clergy involved with this stuff are staggering. Your question isn't difficult. We have centers set up and you take the copy of the hard drive in for them to examine. They particularly want to look at any signs of distribution of the stuff or of sex chat rooms with kids.

Eric stumbled in his thinking. "You mean they really have this sex chat stuff going on with clergy?"

"Yes. If you find a sex chat room, look for a time at the end of the school day or on a snow day off from school. Go into it and you will find these perverts talking about sex to young kids. They make their plans to get together for this sex in the chat rooms. Some kids are forced into this by sadistic parents or guardians. Sadly the priests into this actually save these chats to read them later."

"I'm not sure if they do this or not at St. Charles."

"Come by and get the address from me for the Child Exploitation Division. Who knows what these priests have planned? The damage caused by a few priests presents a huge problem."

The letter came from the diocese telling Luke to go speak with its lawyer, called a chancellor. Sighing as he began trudging toward the lawyer's offices looking for justice, Luke grabbed his brown fedora hat. Was he trying to look like Humphrey Bogart now or was this the way all people on a mission dressed? He walked all the way to K Street and northwest 13th Street. How did a church afford such an extravagant address so close to the White House? Taking the fast elevator up to the ninth floor, after a desultory conversation with the receptionist, Luke walked into the large corner office.

The chancellor for the diocese of Washington sat down across a table from Luke. A tall older man with a black goatee, he was dressed in an expensive suit and when Luke looked at his eyes, he felt like he was in the middle of a freezing blizzard. The chancellor began abruptly, "I looked through the evidence you brought in but I saw only a few small signs of anything unusual. There are only two scenarios here. It could be that the janitor did this. Many times these people from the lower classes sneak downstairs and use the computers when no one is looking. In that situation we let the tech guy change the password and see what happens in the future."

Luke could neither move nor speak.

The chancellor continued, "But the more likely case is this. You have complete access to this computer and I have heard that you have shown signs of instability. The bishop and I believe that you are projecting this evidence on to the good Father Peter. And we think you propositioned men in Stanton Park a month ago."

"That wasn't me. I do not know who it was."

"A St. Charles priest, we have been told. We have evidence it is you."

Luke unexpectedly found himself saying, "Our conscience matters and I am following mine. As a human being, we can take a stand if it matters to us. It matters so much that when we lose our conscience, we say that we have sold our soul to the devil. As

Ignatius said, we can end up in hell with eternal judgment but the opposite is also true."

Luke smiled at the shocked look on the lawyer's face. Luke almost felt sorry for him because the lawyer did not understand this.

Luke stood up, "Good afternoon. Please send this to me in writing."

Chancellor Hugo muttered under his breath, "You and your odd friends can leave the church."

Stunned, Luke continued walking and heard an echoing curse directed at him before the door closed. He slammed his hat on and, face flushed bright red, hit the button calling the elevator. What next? *A strong will*, Ignatius said, *is a sign of healing*. With his own strong will, Ignatius himself had vowed to be of assistance to the pope. For the first time in his life, Luke knew he was on the way to becoming that most extraordinary of creatures: a fulfilled Jesuit. I am not even a Jesuit and I might be defrocked, he laughed to himself, but nonetheless I'll be a Jesuit and somehow Luke knew that Ignatius would approve.

Chapter Ten

What happens when a priest falls? Grabbing, strangling, he tries to take down the others, all in the name of community. Beware, our living host and blood will be touched by evil and explode in despair.

For Luke the forces of war gathered much too slowly. Yet he remembered one idea from seminary over and over again: God is not a domesticated force that struggling human beings order around. God's timing is not our timing.

Out of an Alitalia airline flight, David Sanchez emerged into Dulles airport outside of Washington, DC. His drab gray street clothes and brown briefcase hid his elegant clerical presence and brilliant mind.

In Luke's car driving into the city, David explained, "I'm staying with some colleagues that teach at Georgetown University and telling them I only want to research while I am here. What I won't tell them is that this research is about the depths of depravity in this situation with your diocesan bishop." David grimaced. "Operation Predators. The title works."

Luke's story of recent events tumbled out quickly as he told David what had been happening. "We think Cahill's demanding sex from priests and some are giving in out of fear. And Leo, remember him from our time in Rome? He's part of this."

David pulled up a chair to his office at Georgetown University and picked up the envelope labeled, "Caution: Offensive Materials contained within." David explained, "I requested this from our efficient Eric."

"Let's see what he has found."

Luke took a deep breath and momentarily turned away. He then looked at the first page containing a long series of small pictures. Grotesque image after image leered up at him.

David said, "This is hardcore stuff."

Luke said nothing, his head pounding in pain.

David turned around. His dark eyes did not seem to focus on anything in the room. "I cannot give you easy words about this situation." David's dark eyes shot up quickly to meet Luke's. Then he offered what he could. "The official term for this is cupidity, intense desires for the lower passions of power and pleasure known as evil." He paused. "Yet what is particular about these passions in a priest is that it becomes more than even power and sex—it becomes a lust for hell and bringing others into that mysterious and dreadful reality. What could be more powerful than controlling the destiny of a person's soul? Leo and others saw that if they used their spiritual persuasion to reach the soul as well as the body, the person can become so entangled in darkness that he will never find his way out. The journey into darkness may last for a lifetime, indeed for eternity.

"Only those who have been reared by God have the strength to engage in this type of warfare against destructive forces. These are the ones who have something worth fighting for: the deep satisfaction of God."

David said to Luke, "You have the mind of a warrior. Use it." He continued, "They are trying to destroy you."

Saturday night arrived. Luke and David walked to Jerry's room. Dressed entirely in clerical black, Jerry answered the door, his lips a straight line across his face.

"Father Jerry, this is Father David Hernandez."

Jerry muttered, "Who are you?"

David replied, "Stay on task here, Father. I am going through this with you. Later we have time for explanations."

Jerry's eyes darkened. "Yes" was all he said.

The bishop's residence, two blocks from the Vatican embassy off of Massachusetts Avenue, a stately gray building with the white and yellow square Vatican flag hanging out front, was ready for the Saturday evening party. A round circling driveway allowed drop-off for the church officials visiting the elegant reception. The huge mansion had a full staff of butlers for his required entertaining. Knocking on the door, David and Jerry stood, dressed in full clerical black with their white tab collars. David murmured, "Stay with me."

Inside was an entrance hall with butlers taking coats and putting them away. Jerry saw David watch intently where they were carried. As they turned the corner to go into the large reception room, black-clothed clerics were everywhere, with only an occasional woman presenting herself. A grand piano was sitting in the window with a man playing musical theater show music. When they walked in, the song was, "Listen to the Mockingbird!" Jerry's mouth fell open, but David leaned across and whispered, "No reaction to anything."

Bishop Cahill wore black with a swatch of episcopal purple in the form of a long purple scarf casually thrown around his neck and dangling down past his waist. He immediately walked over to

Jerry, saying, "How good of you to come to one of my little parties!" But then seeing David, his eyes narrowed a bit. "And who is
your distinguished guest?"

Jerry said, a little too loud, "This is a priest from my father's
church in San Francisco. David Hernandez is his name."

Hearing the name of the city, Cahill paused a moment and
said, "Any friend of Jerry's is a friend of mine. I hope you enjoy
yourself."

David put on a small smile. "I intend to. I must say I have
heard of your entertaining but this exceeds all of my expectations.
I am so glad to be a part of all of this." He waited and repeated, "Of
all of this!"

Cahill relaxed and said, "Jerry, I always respected you but
now even more. David sounds like a wonderful addition to our
festivities. Go eat! We have hours. And do wander around upstairs.
Mi casa es su casa. Don't they say that in California?"

"They do indeed, Bishop. How I wish I could have been with
you and your staff on the recent Caribbean cruise!"

The bishop smiled. "You really missed something. Next time,
my friend, I am not leaving port without your handsome presence.
Come and sail away with us!" Laughter greeted the invitation.

As the two walked away, Jerry noticed a steady stream of men
going up and down the stairs. David said, "Prepare yourself, my
friend. What you see tonight will haunt you for a lifetime."

As the piano continued, Jerry reached for the small quiches
and pushed past the squid. An ice sculpture of cowboy boots decorated with lobster and Alaska king crab graced the middle of the
banquet table. A cowboy hat chocolate cake rested on the side with
only a few pieces missing.

Jerry saw well-established priests, known as cardinal rectors,
talking quietly with seminarians dressed in black cassocks, looking like altar boys. Jerry flinched when he saw his friend Tony in
the midst of the group.

"What's with the dress of the seminarians? I've not seen that
at a party before."

"Easier to take off. Enough talk. Tell me about your ministry. Play this straight. The bishop will come ask to show you around soon. Take a deep breath and leave. Then I will follow and interrupt with surprised innocence. We will get out of here. In case anything goes totally astray, use violence. Don't let him get away with anything. We will protect you."

"But who are you?"

"No. Just trust."

"Your ministry. Tell me about your ministry. Focus, Jerry. The best way to combat evil is to focus on the good."

Jerry started in a forced voice, "I love serving at the Lord's table. What does the Scripture say? "One day in your courts is better than a thousand in the world." When I celebrate mass," and Jerry found himself actually feeling lighter, and repeated, "when I celebrate mass, I feel like I have expanded into heaven." David looked at the young priest and Jerry continued, "You know I have a younger sister named Claire. And she writes me letters telling me how proud she is to have an older brother who is a priest. And sometimes before I lead the mass, I thank God for my vocation and how proud Claire is of me."

Then Cahill interrupted with a jolly booming voice. "Here you are! Come, Jerry, let me show you the rooms upstairs."

"Surely, Bishop." And without missing a beat, Jerry turned to leave. The bishop turned to David, "Stay and try the chocolate cake. It is out of this world!"

Cahill led the way up the stairs. Jerry saw a seminarian go into a bedroom; behind were two men who seemed to stand in line at the door. Cahill led Jerry into the next room. An immense bed with a gold and purple bedspread was in the middle. On the huge dresser were various lotions and ointments. Towels lay across the dresser.

A huge crucifix hung above the bed. Cahill drew his attention to it.

"The pope gave this to me when I was consecrated. What a beautiful experience that was! The Roman elegance cannot be beat. A gorgeous ceremony in St. Peter's with priests from all around the globe in attendance. The prayers of the faithful ascending to heaven! I saw cardinals and prayed in humility that one day I could be among them. And afterwards I visited the papal mansion. I hope my small home has just a faint resemblance to it."

Jerry suddenly realized that this was seduction. "He takes me into his bedroom and reminds me what I could have one day." He began to feel nauseated.

"And afterwards, the parties with the grand Italian food and dignitaries. The press wrote about the whole glorious day, a day that included Scripture and God and rich food and wine and a wonderful all-night party."

Jerry stood without moving. An orgy, he thought.

"But you know, my boy, there are other wonderful experiences waiting you in the church. God does not expect us to be perfect but only willing to confess and ask for forgiveness. And I know that I am forgiven and purified every time I confess." Cahill began to take off his purple scarf and began to pull it back and forth in his hands. Back and forth. Back and forth. Then he kissed the scarf and touched it tenderly. He tied it around his neck and slowly began to untie it. Pulling it through his fingers, he whispered, "These hands of mine have embraced the holy elements and now will embrace yours." He began to place the scarf around Jerry's waist. Jerry wondered, *is it time to do something?* when he heard the locked door trying to open.

In relief, Jerry heard the doorknob tried. "Excuse me, Jerry, are you in there?" David shouted.

"I'm here."

"I am sorry to interrupt but your cell phone just rang and I heard it. Unfortunately it was your mother who called to say that Claire has been in an accident and needs to talk to you."

The bishop frowned but then whispered, "Dear Jerry, come back as soon as you can."

"Surely, Bishop."

Then the bishop paused, looked in the mirror to see how he looked. He wiped his flushed cheeks. Placing the purple scarf around his neck, he opened the door.

"Your vigilance is very interesting, Father David."

"Sorry, Bishop, but I saw the number and realized that is was Jerry's parents, who I know well."

With an irritated voice, Cahill said, "Very well. Next time we will gather all cell phones at the door. The Holy Father knows we need relaxation."

Early the next morning, Luke drove David back to the airport. The subdued theologian and canon lawyer said little except, "Let me talk to my superiors about what I have seen. The name of the game now is evidence. Let me repeat that, we need all the evidence we can find to convict Cahill."

Luke sighed. "It seems like our bishop is like the gangster, along with his fallen priests."

"*Discern*," Ignatius proclaimed, "*to avoid having your eternal soul cut off from the heavenly presence of God.*"

This interior gift of discernment works because demons leave behind an invisible footprint. When desolation happens, beware! When demons walk around, they bring temptations and fears. Demons bring desolation; angels bring consolation. In noticing these invisible footprints, wisdom arrives.

Ignatius talked of these realities of consolation and desolation as guides on the way. Remember the enemy's target is not the body or even the mind, but prayer and spirituality because through these arrive a flowing source of life. Once prayers stop, the enemy has won.

Gradually Luke felt a rising conviction. All of this empathy towards transgressing priests must stop and concern must be shown for the victims. He needed to confront influential priests and help powerless kids.

Eric saw an email with the heading "Pornography." The FBI had answered his question about a priest looking at underage children.

Eric quickly began to scan the message and saw lots of good information. "The thing to look for is participation in chat rooms and other online forums where the child porn is traded. I did not see any evidence of that kind of online chat room activity. These online forums are run by organized crime inside and outside of the US. Getting approved by criminals to be in these forums takes some work to prove that you are not law enforcement, and often you need contact with real persons associated with the ring of criminals."

At least they responded to me, Eric thought. He shook his head. *What's next?*

There was confusion at both ends of this email.

Dan talked to his assistant. Tapping his hand on the table, "So much of this filth out there: as soon as the Cherry Blossom Festival is over, we will get back to them."

The younger woman looked at him. "Why the Cherry Blossom Festival? What is the significance of this beyond the beautiful trees and loads of tourists?"

"Two reasons: the mayor is frightened with the IMF meetings coming up that something weird could be coming that could cause international embarrassment or even worse. Could these pinwheel kooks be building toward some murder or occult ceremony with this odd carved symbol? The blood left behind in the parks could mean they are building up to a human sacrifice." Dan shook his head. "Sadly, a lot of child prostitution takes place during the Cherry Blossom Festival. People come from out of town and bring their illegal desires with them so we monitor this problem very carefully." He paused and then added quietly, "I know. My wife is a specialist in this."

His forehead lined and wrinkled, Dan tiptoed into Melora's room. She lay under her Tinkerbell blanket surrounded by her pillow pets, her latest fad where pillows turned into stuffed animals during the day.

"This is dreadful, Annie," Dan muttered, wishing he could talk to his undercover wife. *Where are you? Are you safe or not?*

Then more memories.

"No really, Dan," she had said. "I will stop the undercover work soon. Let me finish this last assignment. You know during Cherry Blossom time all the predators come out in droves looking for underage kids. You know that many of these kids come from southeast DC and I can move in those communities easily. I look like them and can help in a dangerous situation. I'll be gone for a few weeks and then, voila—back here safe and sound."

Dan shook his head no. "These people will stop at nothing, Annie. And we want another baby. Stand up to the bureau. They will let you out of it."

But his strong-willed Annie said no to him, and Dan knew that maybe this was the reason he loved her so much.

He sat on the floor and thought not one more awful video would he watch with the same hellish scene where dead-looking men abuse children.

Something inside of him screamed, "No more!"

Then Melora turned over and reached sleepily for her cat. She opened her eyes, "You did come, Daddy. Is Mommy home yet?"

Dan knew his whole life now rested on that question.

He answered, "Not yet, but soon, Mel. Soon."

Could he abandon those kids out there even now, with criminals ruining their lives and pocketing the profits from their destruction? What would his wife Annie want him to do now besides soldier on through all of this?

Find these criminals. I will do everything I can to take them down as fast as I can. Inside his heart came the words, *Annie, I promise you. I will do everything I can.*

"Night-night, Honey. Sweet dreams."

Melora turned her head towards her cat and fell asleep.

Sighing, Dan wondered: why did someone named Eric keep contacting him about pornography at St. Charles' Parish?

On Saturday evening, a sign announced "A Luau for St. Charles." Peter walked around dressed in a Hawaiian shirt with bright pink and orange hibiscus flowers and multi-colored orchid lei. Leo walked in his clerical blacks but with a serene white orchid pinned below his white clergy collar.

Oscar saw Bishop Cahill heading into the party and broke into song. "It's me, it's me, O Lord, standing in the need of prayer!" Bishop Cahill turned and looked steadily at Oscar, who promptly sang another round of his energetic song.

Walking over to get rare steak shish-ka-bob, Leo stopped to chat with General Knight when Oscar walked over and smiled at Leo. During a quiet moment, Oscar looked at Leo and sang boldly, "Listen to the mockingbird! Singing over her grave!" Quiet greeted his dramatic rendition and faithful parishioners who knew the singer's familiar ways, clapped when he finished. Yet Leo flushed and started to walk away, except the flower-bedecked Peter who had quickly walked over and placed his hand on his arm. Peter murmured, "He means no harm."

As the guests were leaving, Leo walked over to Peter.

"So what's up with the vocalist at St. Charles?"

Peter looked at the parish's carefully set clock. A second passed, now another, now another.

Peter tried to soothe Leo. "Look, that's the only way Oscar can talk."

Leo responded, "Such compassion, Father."

Peter ignored the taunting.

"A stroke destroyed part of his mind, Leo. It could happen to any of us."

Leo stood straighter.

"Stay away from him," Peter said quietly. "He's my . . ."

"Your friend," Leo finished. "He's a menace to our order." Tick-tock. Tick-tock. Tick-tock.

Chapter Eleven

What happens when a priest falls? Slowly at first, the infection begins and then with an exploding desolation, interior faith is eaten by forces not of God.

Luke went to his mailbox at the church and saw that the official diocesan letter had finally showed up in his mailbox. Had the clowns been sent in?

Luke's hand shook as he took out the heavy, formal stationery. Tearing into it, he stood stunned. The letter was from the bishop. "You are herewith suspended from all liturgical duties while we perform an investigation." The letter offered no explanation and ended with the lame detail that his pay would continue for at least one more month but he should now be making alternative plans.

Late at night Luke lay in his small room in the rectory. *So my suspension is because they think I was that priest caught in the park soliciting sex with somebody. Or at least they say they think I was the priest, but I am the scapegoat for someone else. Who could that be?*

Then like a gift from Ignatius, Luke thought, *why attack me? Cahill and Leo had attacked me from behind and beaten me up before I even knew I was in a fight.*

Luke grabbed the Fifth Exercise. *I need to learn to fight the way I can.*

The heading announced:

"It is a meditation on hell."

Who wants to think about this? Who even believes in it? Luke read: "The goal is "here to see with the sight of the imagination the length, breadth and depth of Hell." To hear the wailings, cries, and blasphemies. To see the great fires and the souls as in bodies of fire, to gain the interior sense of the pain the damned suffer. And our Commanding officer Ignatius ordered, *"The first Exercise will be made at midnight.""*[1]

There were so many gentler and simpler saints, Luke thought. Why not a smiling Mother Teresa or a serene Julian of Norwich? Why this commanding soldier Ignatius? Luke grumbled to himself. The clock said 11:30 p.m. and he knew it was time to go to the church to think about hell.

At midnight Luke walked into the completely darkened church to meditate on hell, a place of torment and punishment named after infant sacrifice where some had taken their newborn babies to sacrifice to Moloch.

But who can think of hell? Shocked, Luke realized that all thoughts of hell are from grace and then grace answered by images of endless torment filtering in Luke's postmodern consciousness with images of screaming, violent, wandering, hopeless people; hell, where blasphemies were screamed out, "If you are the Son of God, come down from that cross." Hell where no word of consolation or comfort ever reaches. Hell with the complete absence of hope. Hell where corruption rots and decays and yet the bizarre and twisted souls still exist and scream obscenities and plead for oblivion that never arrives. Hell where . . . and Luke had had enough.

He stood tall and realized the time-tested truth: *They can kill my body but not my soul. Ignatius, I see something of what you saw. I choose life and decide for God.*

1. Ignatius of Loyola, *Spiritual Exercises,* 142.

Jerry sat and prayed that his muse would return; it had been a long time. Quickly the words spurted out. The alpha male wolf cares and commands: the alpha wolf is established as powerful, the one who leads the pack, the one chosen for protection and fighting and wisdom. Now our Alpha Bishop has grown weary and sits looking at the other wolves, not to save them, but to use them for himself. This alpha wants only his own pleasure and dominance as all-powerful and all-demanding. This alpha must go.

But what is this? The she-wolf nudges another male. Challenge, she says. Fight or we will all die. Look at our alpha lying in the sun taking his leisure and pleasure.

The fight! Look at the fight! All the wolves keep their distance and watch. The new male attacks and the quickly overpowers the lazy wolf. Soon the wounded former alpha runs away squealing and destroyed. The pack surrounds the new alpha male and a new day begins.

Jerry walked over to the window. A new alpha must arise or we will all die. The predators exploit and take all the new life we have.

Hannah moved quickly around her small apartment kitchen, expertly tearing up lettuce leaves, cutting tomatoes, melting butter in a frying pan, and throwing in cut-up square of stale bread to make homemade croutons, while Luke sliced a pineapple.

Hannah spoke quickly. "We are stuck, short of contacting *The Washington Post* and becoming a circus of media events that will probably make us look like a Punch and Judy show."

Her words flew out. "So you are suspended and the FBI knows and the bishop knows and Peter knows. What else can we do?"

"We pray now, Hannah."

Suddenly her face contorted. "You're wrong!" she yelled and threw the salad bowl on the floor. "We have got to do something."

Stunned, Luke saw Hannah break into tears and sob, "I'm sorry! I'm sorry! What in the hell is prayer going to do?"

Then she took a full ripe tomato and threw it on the floor and stomped it and watched the red juice and seeds squirt everywhere. A river of red juice raced everywhere with one stream running downhill. Soon the bloody-red juice made a lazy stream toward the place under the refrigerator. She quickly leaned over to get a garbage bag to capture it.

Weeping, Hannah said, "We might be wrong, Father. That minister Mr. Golightly when I was young used to say we give our lives to Jesus Christ, he called it surrender. And I have tried to do it now and look what has happened.

"That minister was wrong! I have been lied to and now we've lost everything."

His eyes also full, Luke stared at her. "Were we wrong?" he reached out and touched her arm. "Maybe we are meant to lose everything. And don't ask me why I said that; I don't know why I said that."

Hannah stared at him.

"You have it, Hannah. That tomato you just destroyed and stomped is our heart and God is stomping it open."

He reached for his notebook and wrote, showing it to Hannah.

7. God tests us by tearing us apart and throwing us on the floor and stomping us. Then truth cries out!

Then laughter broke out, consumed them, and throwing themselves on the kitchen floor, they both cried and laughed, while the red-blood river of tomato juice continued seeking the lowest place.

The next day Luke staggered out of bed and ran to write Hannah an email. He wrote it quickly. "I had this dream last night that you, Eric, and I were sitting around this perfectly circular table and we were reading the signs of God. The signs were like a huge stone tablet written in a symbolic language and we read them simultaneously with both our eyes and our hands. We could not read it quickly but it required great intensity of effort. And together as we did this there was great power released. So I feel like the Spirit is acting in ways beyond our comprehension. We must keep seeking understanding about the actions of God. Even to engage in this work, we release spiritual forces we do not understand."

Bishop Cahill buzzed about his office, looking at his diocesan map. Taking out his ruler, he drew the next line in his complex pinwheel figure. The next line ran straight through Anacostia.

The therapy group met to make plans.

Hudson started, "Ok, enough St. Charles stories. I am sick of them."

Luke looked at his feet. "I can agree with you there, brother. Yet we are living it."

Jerry stood up, his head almost hitting the low ceiling. "I have thought this through."

"Any prayers with those thoughts, Father?" Hudson teased.

"A few." Then taking a deep breath, "We are all going to write letters to the Vatican, at least those of us that can find the courage."

Luke gulped. "Are we going to enclose a case of wine with each letter to stop the priest reading it from hyperventilating?"

Jerry shook his head.

"No, actually I was not accurate when describing what we are doing to do." He stopped and waited for the derisive priests to stop making disrespectful noises. "Actually two of us will write now. We will give this a month and then the final two will write if necessary. And our suspended friend here will write first, because after all, what does he have to lose?"

Jerry announced, "What we are doing is a liturgy."

More groans met him. "This is not a mass," said Luke quietly.

Hudson got it and said elegantly, "Jerry knows the original meaning of the word. A liturgy is a public service conducted at a private cost. The ancient Greeks started this: if you have some excellence within you, then divinity wants you to exercise this gift, yet this is not conducted for money from others, but at your own cost."

Luke exclaimed, "I get it."

"Wait, Luke," Jerry continued. "I need to speak. Wolves have three passions. They rendezvous, den, and hunt like nomads. Wolves care deeply for their children and raise them to be hunters. They stay with their young in the spring in the den until the pup is big enough to hunt to find food. Now humans have become so disordered that tormented people mix it all together. Some monsters mate with our kids, as evil as it is. Some become our kids' predators. We destroy our own. And you think these suffering children don't deserve our letters? They deserve our lives."

Luke leaned forward quickly. "I'll write!" he said enthusiastically.

The ideas flowing quickly, Jerry asserted, "We need to tell them that this isn't sex for love or even pleasure. This is sex to bring in the demons and let them control the church. We need to make sure that we say this in our letters."

Bruce chimed in, "Dropping like flies!"

Groans abound.

He quickly added, "We could resign en masse?"

Hudson replied. "And self-destruct like a flash in the pan? Not for me."

Jerry, "Okay, okay, bros."

Hudson shot back, "And where did you get the jail language, Father?"

"From my visits to the DC jail, homey. To survive in that extremely tough place the inmates have a word for everything. But forgive me—I don't wish to offend you."

Then following this apology, Luke jumped in, "So what is the problem here? Does anyone know what is really going on?"

A few heads nodded yes. Jerry began, "Or at least we think so. There's a list the bishop is working on and it seems chaotic. My friend in Rockville got a reception invitation, a party invitation, and then a private meeting."

Everyone stiffened.

"He said no, but some do not. Increasing physical demands and then after that you are part of the quiet, initiated tribe."

Slumping over, heads everywhere looked at the floor but Jerry's unusually insistent voice added, "If you refuse, you are accused of financial or sexual impropriety or mental problems. Cahill seems to pull the charges out of the air and then plant the evidence. The more you protest your innocence, the worse you appear.

"Our challenge is huge. The domination accomplished by the bonding of shame caused by these rapes is practically indestructible."

Hudson quietly asked, "What would make me write a letter and identify myself to the Pontificate as a complaining priest?"

Luke began, "Ignatius said . . ." when Jerry interrupted.

"Not this time."

Jerry leaned over and stared at Hudson directly.

"I don't care who your uncle is—to move up you have to get attention from the hierarchy somehow. So think this through: we report a predator bishop, get help, and you have put up with it. You'll be seen as Cahill's enabler or even a predator yourself.

"But if you report, you might be seen as a courageous, up-and-coming cleric."

Hudson snorted. "I don't take you seriously. Who do you know?"

"Luke has contacts in Rome. That's all I'll say."

"Tell me who."

"No, you choose the risk you want to take."

Accurately Bruce concluded, "The risk of reporting with outspoken priests or the risk of siding with sexual predators. But if we report it and the hierarchy agrees with us, then I can see the cardinals thinking that what you have inside isn't quite the right stuff."

Confidently, Jerry said, "All roads lead to Rome, Hudson. You will find your way to the justice and glory of Rome or the orgies and degradation of Rome. You choose."

With a steely coolness, Jerry called for the question, "So how many will write?"

Luke and Bruce's hand went up. A long pause with no response from Hudson.

He looked straight ahead. "Not yet, friends. Let me think about this."

Ignoring him, Jerry said, "We have had enough. Let's write the letters out of our convictions and not share them with each other until they are finished. We want each letter to be written from our hearts and not sound like group creations. And fly them off to Rome, brothers, and soon."

As they left, a vulture tore at the dead squirrel in front of the Vatican embassy.

Jerry squinted, "Look!"

The group turned, and with questioning eyes turned toward him.

"Ancient Rome looked upon vultures as divine creatures because they never kill to eat but clean the earth up of dead animals. In fact, vultures will never even eat dead birds, an animal of their own species: they have standards for what they eat."

The black vulture turned to look at the men.

Bruce muttered, "This gives me the chills. What's next, Jerry, oracles?"

Jerry merely responded, "Next? The power of Rome continues." Suddenly serious, he whispered, "Brothers, this might be our only chance to understand God. Go for it! If we fail, we'll become busboys at a La Madeleine restaurant, but we've tried. We've tried. That in itself is noble."

That evening Hudson called his uncle, the Philadelphia cardinal, and left a voice message. "I am part of a group of priests that needs watching. They are planning on creating havoc—I can't tell you for good or bad. Please call me back."

And in the diocesan offices, the same question roiled the atmosphere. Leo's eyelids fluttered, and then, "A pinwheel, Bishop?" His throat choking, his voice momentarily shook.

Making a clucking sound, the bishop responded rapidly. "Yes, a pinwheel; don't you get it?"

His zooming words sped out. "Like Zorro! Can't you see the good we are doing? Creating a group of priests that are all part of a select group and connected to me? We are all for one and one for all." Then in a softer voice, the bishop continued, "I never made cardinal, but my work will last forever. Let those cardinals keep their red hats; I have personally created a tribe of committed priests."

The bishop's hands moved expansively in revolving orbits. "One day our brilliance will be recognized and this diocese will blaze with glory. Our glorious deeds will live forever!"

Leo looked away. He was a long way from Rome now and maybe this was the American spin. What do the Americans say in situations like these? Whatever.

As Cahill strode toward the door, "Leo, don't you know this symbol? And you are from Rome?"

Leo, scowling, headed toward the nearest computer to start his frantic search.

Chapter Twelve

What happens when a priest falls? Leaving prayer far behind, death grows and grows and grows. How will this end? Tearing apart the fabric of goodness, they dwell in living horror, for their weeping victims rest in the living hand of God.

Without the leadership of Dr. Wagner, the group had no compulsion to attend but Wednesday afternoon arrived and all the members strode in.

Bruce started, "So what is wrong with the priesthood now?"

Luke stammered as he searched for the ideas. "A few of these popular and successful ministries are run by priests who have worked out an intricate and interior reward system that involves corruption. If I do this, I will have another affair or buy a person or drink all I can. They hide this as long as they can, but it always gets out."

General assent greeted his statement and then they jumped to the chase.

Jerry muttered, "The essence of the wolf is protection of its own lived in community. It takes one Roman to know another. I know what Cahill is doing." The other priests waited quietly.

He continued, "Cahill rewards himself with the destruction of priests. He is a predator in more ways than one. He feeds on watching priest after priest fall under the power of his charm. Then he pulls back and watches them fall. Leo, Cahill, and a couple of other priests are having orgies with the seminarians."

Bruce interrupted, "So you want to hear my letter?" Eyes open, all quietly nodded their heads affirmatively.

""We are living in pure terror in the diocese of Washington because of our unstable bishop who looks for sexual partners from the rank of priests. We need help right away. We are dropping like flies!""

Spontaneously everyone laughed. "You can't keep that dead bug metaphor out, can you, Bruce?" Hudson murmured.

Jerry said quietly, "You know what Aristotle said: the creation of a metaphor is a sign of genius."

Hudson spoke, "I never heard that quote before, but the letter lacks sophistication."

Bruce blurted, "We don't need sophistication; we need help! That will get their attention."

Luke smiled. "That it will." He continued, "Mine begins:

""The church has lost its way in the diocese of Washington and we need immediate assistance from the Vatican to remove our predator Bishop Cahill.""

"Jerry, do you want to share?"

Jerry began, ""My beloved Pope Francis, Father Bishops and Cardinals, and my Brother Priests:

Our beloved Saint Augustine of Hippo is oft quoted as "Love God and do what you like." This means that the love of God changes our hearts and minds and souls followed by an interior freedom. What a beautiful spiritual understanding this admonition gives us. Yet in the diocese of Washington, our bishop follows with great abandon the second portion of this command without the wisdom and discernment of the first. In short, we have a bishop who cares not about the purifying love of God. Instead, he seeks and commands sensual satisfaction from those priests serving under him, meaning of course that he dominates diocesan priests with his sexual demands.""

General affirmation greeted his letter.

"Hudson, what about you?"

"Not yet decided," came his noncommittal reply. "Is this really true and or is this group hysteria?"

Bruce accused, "You've told your uncle we are crazy."

"Maybe, maybe not."

Later that evening after he returned to his prominent rectory near Embassy Row, Hudson saw the handwritten note lying on his large oak desk.

"Meet me tonight at Anacostia Park at 10 pm." The note was signed simply, "Cahill."

Wondering, Hudson carefully reached for the message and pondered, *What does this mean?* But maybe the bishop was coming out after an evening meeting and had some church news to relate to him. Hudson quickened as he thought that maybe he would hear about that bishop's position in North Carolina.

Later in the beautiful spring evening, Hudson headed out to the park located over the Sousa Bridge off of Pennsylvania Avenue with a lazy, curving road descending to the park. Leaving his car, he saw the spacious open area now empty of children, picnickers, and the occasional drugdealer. Sailboats and yachts drifted gently in the water, an empty bike path clung to the shoreline, and Canadian geese strutted around in large groups. The park lay off of the Anacostia River, and after recent development, the area was now graced with an elaborate swing and slide playground, with picnic tables and open green fields.

"Come down by the river!" he heard Cahill's jolly voice call out to him.

Hudson turned and saw Cahill on the bike path dressed in blue jeans accentuating his heavy stomach, a red bandana, a blue shirt, and a black baseball cap. Slowly he walked down to meet Cahill.

"Son, it's time to talk about that new bishopric. You know it's time and I have to recommend someone to Rome soon. So I thought it a beautiful evening for a stroll along the Anacostia. It's a quiet place to meet and a way to help out the distressed Anacostia area."

Hudson and Cahill started their slow stroll away from civilization.

"North Carolina is a great diocese and an important position with possibilities of more promotions."

Hudson agreed, "I am interested and think I have a vocation to the episcopate."

"The church needs leaders like you."

Hudson flushed: so close now to where he wanted to be. He wanted to grab the possibility and run with it.

Sensing this, Cahill waved a lazy arm at the playground.

"Hey, have you ever seen the pirate's ship?" A new frown appeared between Hudson's eyes and he turned to his left to see the huge playground equipment, an immense red pirate ship with floating white sails lurking near a hill close to the river.

Irritated at the change in conversation, Hudson shrugged, "No. A little unusual, though. I have never seen a pirate ship as playground equipment."

"Plenty of open space below deck. And look at all the cannons poking out everywhere. They even have fake cannonballs inside. And that skull-and-crossbones flag at the top. Fabulous."

With Hudson slowly trailing behind, without an explanation Cahill started walking toward the fifty-feet long ship and said, "Actually, Father, want a cigarette?"

"No, of course not—I mean, no thank you."

Cahill strode into the boat and then yelled, "Don't be shy, Hudson. Come on in!"

As in a dream, Hudson followed.

Cahill placed his Vatican knife on the top of the interior cannon and took out a small whip and started twirling it around in the air.

"Time to walk the plank, Father! Let's take off some of those uncomfortable clothes, partner! More pirates will be here soon."

"Is this a joke, bishop?" But as Cahill picked up the whip and walked toward him, Hudson started backing out of the door, mouth open. With Hudson nearly gone, Cahill lunged at him, grabbing his disappearing shoulders.

"Not so fast, son! Think of it; purple shirts, red robes, honor from around the globe, gobs of money, and all the sex you want!"

Hudson cursed at him quietly, trying to shake the bishop's hands off and again started backing out the door.

"Think you know all the right people, sport? I'll show you what you need!"

Cahill took out his whip and began licking it at the priest and Hudson's cheeks showed some lightly bleeding pirate scars with one deep wound gushing red blood right above his left eye. Cahill quickly reached out and wiped off the blood dripping down Hudson's face.

"Now are you ready? Pirates and pleasure!"

And Hudson lunged back at Cahill with all his strength, pushing him down and heard the bishop's head hit a plastic cannon. As Hudson ran out the door, he heard an echoing curse from the fallen bishop.

Back in his room, Hudson ran for his phone, dialed his uncle, and got the familiar voice message.

"Uncle!" he cried out, "I need your help! I am in terrible trouble!"

He sat down, chest still heaving, and then almost against his will, he yelled. "Don't tell me that crazy Bruce is right!"

Then, "At least I had been warned about this." And Hudson sat hour after hour waiting for his cardinal uncle to call and to tell him the whole seamy story.

About two that morning, the call arrived and Hudson told the cardinal what happened.

The older man responded, "Are you sure? You say that Cahill took you to a pirate's ship?" His uncle's skeptical tone awoke Hudson's passion.

"Yes, he did." Adding with emphasis, "A plastic red pirate's ship in Anacostia Park in Washington, DC. This whole diocese is living in terror. Who do we report this to? What can we do?"

The uncle cleared his throat. "Let me take this back to my brother cardinals."

As Hudson put down the phone, he frowned, thinking, "Now I see where my careful, reticent qualities come from."

The next morning on WTOP news: "The mystery of park vandalism continues with new symbols carved in the pirate's ship at Anacostia Park." A pause continued by, then the announcer laughed and spontaneously added, "Call our talk-back line and let us know if you knew that Washington, DC had a pirate's ship on a kids' playground." Cutting off his microphone, the announcer groaned. What made him do that? This whole story was so weird and ridiculous, but maybe his son would enjoy seeing this new crime scene. Unbelievable.

On his way to work, Leo heard the news on the radio. Seeing the bishop's dour expression when he walked in, Leo decided it was time to spring the news. He began, "I have a choice tidbit for you: a beautiful thirteen-year-old boy, successful in school and headed toward a great future when he becomes one with us. His mother has been compromised by Peter. We are all set." Pause, and then emphasized his point. "I planned this just for you!"

The atmosphere became close.

Leo laughed, "He won't know what has happened until it is over."

The bishop whispered, "Start it now. How do you do it these days?"

Leo whispered back, "So easy with texts. This will happen right with the Cherry Blossom Festival. Beautiful."

Andrew's phone began the familiar bongs signifying a new text.

"Did u c see the site? Cool. Huh?"

An hour later.

"Ofc ik the ppl in it surprised u, but its funny !: P."

Another hour later and with Andrew's head swimming now.

"Hey did u hear Robert and Paula are partners? Such fun!"

Sixty minutes later and the clock is ticking until Andrew implodes.

"I'm planning a party with some making out. I'll bring other kids."

Andrew imagined that pretty Ashley he had been watching at the confirmation class. Sure, he wanted that.

And later that night, the phone clanged again.

"U are so handsome and I am proud to know u. Let's hang out and hook up sometime."

Andrew's trembling hands texted back. "OK." He wanted to be popular on top of being successful and if that girl was going to be there, he was going too.

Quickly then, "Parks in the evening are fun. I'll tell your mother you are attending an all-night retreat weekend as you consider the priesthood."

The next morning, another text noisily clanged in.

This one announced, "I am on Cloud Nine!"

Andrew's mind pondered this. Maybe all kids need to lie to their mothers to get a life, and having such an influential friend as Leo could really help with these college applications.

But something bothered him: what does "hook up" mean?

Eric's caller ID announced a call from Kevin and, lunging across the desk, he grabbed it.

"I have the information for you. The organization you need to call is the Washington Field Office of the FBI in Manassas, Virginia.

"My contact said to call the Complaint Desk at the Innocent Images National Initiative Crimes Against Children."

Eric called the number.

"I have evidence that on the priests' computer at St. Charles, they are looking at pornography, possibly involving children, and I had sent in copies of the hard drive."

The professional answer came back quickly. "Have you directly observed this?"

"No. But I copied the hard drive with the images on it."

"If you sent it in, we already have it. We will get in touch with you if we need to."

"Okay. What is your name?"

"I don't give out my name for security purposes but here is the email address. We will make sure that it gets to the right person."

Jerry dreamed that he stood at a distance and watched a huge fire leaping like a geyser, squirting up in giant flames. Out of the fire calmly walked exotic animals: a gorgeous lion, an elegant tiger, and three gray wolves. As he watched, he saw the animals begin to walk towards him, yet as they walked their original shapes metamorphosed into those of huge wolves. Gradually more and more attack wolves appeared and took their places in a military formation. The fire continued but now no more shapes appeared from it. Jerry grabbed for his paper and started writing.

Leo had the waiting basement room all ready. He had the cameras waiting and a script for this shoot. He waited for the arrival of Bishop Cahill. They had planned for this night for months.

Cahill left his palatial rectory dressed in unusually tight blue jeans and cowboy boots. Enough with these purple and silver crosses, he wanted some real living. He got in his black Cadillac and started to go to the rendezvous. Wow, there was nothing better than absolution tomorrow from Leo. All of those priests were pretty good too, and their reluctance to do this added to the pleasure.

But now, let the good times roll. Let's have a warm-up for this memorable evening. He headed over to Dupont Circle, a happening area. He circled the roundabout several times and saw two good-looking young men sitting in the active circle near the spurting fountain, dressed in tight pants, looking open to suggestions. "Hey, guys, are you both open for adventure. I got some extra cash today." They walked over to the car. "How much are we worth to you?" Cahill paused, looking them up and down. "How about two hundred a piece?" They opened the door and put their heads in the window. "Come on out, Pops." They flipped open their badges. "DC police." Hustling the bishop into the back of the police car, Cahill watched the elegant Embassy Row disappear into the distance as he approached the tough jail district.

Soon southeast Washington, DC came into focus and Cahill saw the Robert F. Kennedy Stadium outside of the window in the back of the police car. He already imagined what he would do. Get hold of Leo through the quick phone call allowed to prisoners, describe this terribly mistaken communication, bail himself out quietly, sic his lawyer on these ignorant police, and it's over. Rome will never know. Yet his bravado failed as he saw the DC jail: a huge fortress without windows, an overcrowded inmate population made up almost entirely from southeast DC (the poor Ward Eight which Cahill never visited). One of his too-diligent priests once suggested advocating to the mayor about the dreadful conditions at the DC jail, yet Cahill nixed that because he socialized with the DC mayor who would be offended. Cahill desperately tried to reach the busy Leo but his cell phone was off. He called and left a message for the diocesan chancellor. But after being photographed, fingerprinted, and deprived of personal belongings, the correctional officers had Cahill dressed in a too-tight, bright orange jumpsuit. He was escorted to a crowded open room full of inmates. "Hey, paunchy! That garb doesn't work for you." "Hey, isn't that the bishop whose picture is in the *Post* all the time?" "What did you do to get in here?" "Rape a kid?" someone suggested. And they started to surround him while the few guards present hid themselves behind their fully extended newspapers.

The first inmate took the heel of his hand and hit him on the back of the head. Cahill suddenly gasped in pain and his torment had only begun.

But soon the officials came in and seeing the older man's weakened condition, hustled him into protective custody. Finally Leo responded, made an outraged call to the mayor's office, and whisked him back home for needed R & R.

The mayor picked up his phone, called the police chief, and said in a raised tone, "How in the world could your police take the Catholic bishop to the DC jail?"

The chief sat. Then, "He might be guilty."

The mayor pushed, "Look—I am a personal friend of Bishop Cahill. This is a mistake that I don't want to happen again. We have leaders of the known world coming here for the IMF meeting and weird blogs trying to incite riots from the college students and you pick up Cahill?"

Anxious to change the subject, the chief offered solid IMF details, "We have the limousine routes planned down to the detail and motorcycle police ready to stop all traffic to keep these leaders safe. Street closures will be absolute and final so that they make meetings in time and enjoy their parties."

Then the mayor stated, "And who are the nuts doing the pinwheels?"

"I think a New Age group in Adams-Morgan. The pinwheel has some meaning for them about universal peace or something in the future. We have them under surveillance."

"Good." And the mayor reached for his needed stomach medicine.

Luke had come to a dead end in his spirit about all of this. "I have protested as much as I can," he said.

He walked by Leo sitting in his office, his black clerical outfit looking professional, his hair recently groomed, carrying on a quiet phone conversation. How do you describe depravity? As Luke looked in, Leo looked up and Luke knew how to describe this now. Leo's face showed no concern or worry; the lines of his middle age seemed normal. But his eyes were frightening in their flatness. No passion, love, joy, or laughter, as if Leo's soul was in such conflict with his lusts that the soul had packed up and left. He looked almost like a corpse propped in the office pretending to be alive. And that deadness was something Luke would run to the ends of the earth to avoid. Or maybe just run directly to Saint Ignatius.

Eric texted, "They haven't contacted me, Aunt Hannah. I am really bothered by this. We put all that evidence together and they don't seem to think that this is important enough and they told us to approach the church authorities, as if we had not already done that before."

"No news, Hannah . . . im rlly annoyed. we worked hard 2 get the stuff 2gether but they told us 2 tlk 2 the church authorities. duhh!

Ugh, can't believe it! What next? & now ppl will b hurt?

wat can we do now?! cant think of anything :(

Hannah responded and texted back, "I can't believe this! What now and how many innocent people will be hurt?"

nothing. lost everything. Hope church doesnt hurt ur career . . . srry this happened! <3

Eric continued, "What can we do now? I can't think of a thing."

"Nothing. We have lost everything. I just hope the church doesn't chase you and hurt your career. I am so sorry that I got you into this!"

The journey into darkness continues.

Chapter Thirteen

What happens when a priest falls? Does he fall like Lucifer from the presence of God, cast down, and feeling God's beauty slip away every second? All he can hear is the roar of anxiety as he falls into a darkness like no other, whose heaviness he hears and whose lost-ness he tastes? The beatific vision fades and no other vision arises and all that is there is his rotting soul that breaks away in huge dying clumps even as he moves. All that stands before him is need and nothingness.

Luke walked over to the rectory and out of the shadows walked an attractive, African American woman in her twenties, wearing bright coral lipstick, long gold earrings, and huge high heels. Without a greeting, she said, "Where's Leo?"

Luke turned to look at her. "I don't know. I haven't seen him today."

"When is he getting back?"

"I don't know."

"Look, don't be withholding information from me. The next time I'm with him, I'll complain about you."

Luke just looked and said with emphasis, "I don't know where he is or when he will be back." He quickly let himself into the rectory.

The woman looked at him through the window and taunted him. "You think that is going to help you?" And she backed away into the dark garden.

Suddenly walking around the corner of the building, Oscar broke into, "O Shenandoah, I long to hear you! Away, you rolling river!"

That evening Peter returned and invited Oscar into the expansive kitchen.

"Hi, Oscar. I had a long meeting today and missed seeing you. How is everything?"

Oscar sang, "List to the mocking bird! List to the mocking bird!" Oscar stumbled over the listen word and it came out as a one syllable "list." Peter looked at him and enunciated the word carefully for him, saying "Listen." Oscar looked at him with softened eyes.

Oscar sang it again. "List to the mocking bird!" Peter walked over to the rectory kitchen and looked for the Lady Finger cookies that Oscar liked. He put two on a plate and gently guided his singer to the table. Oscar limply raised one cookie, tasted it, put it down, and then started singing again, "List to the mockingbird!" Oscar stammered over and over again.

Jerry walked in. "What's wrong with him, Monsignor? It sounds like he is trying to say your name."

Peter's answer came softly. "I am afraid he is developing health issues and cannot remember the words of his songs. If his music disappears, then . . ." And Peter stopped, his hand reaching out for Oscar's shoulder with a gentle tap.

"Time for sleep! You will feel better tomorrow."

Oscar fell into bed. He sang his usual night song, "God rest you merry gentlemen!" but still restless, he closed his eyes. He heard a sound of wood grating and then sat up to look up at the door. He tried to yell, but the song sprang out, "Up on the housetop, reindeer paws!"[1] when the sound of breaking glass behind his head, the potent hammer angrily flew through the open window, knocked open his skull and Oscar fell out, his brains breaking loose from his shattered skull, his fingers crumpled on the floor, his head hanging at a freakish angle, his body still seeming to seek sleep and with this, the end of the singing, praying genius. His brains and blood swam in chaotic patterns all over on the floor of the St. Charles rectory.

Holy mother of God, what is this? thought Luke as he ran down the stairs. Oscar lay on his back, the top of his head scalped off surrounded in a pool of blood that dripped bit by bit down the stairs. Luke sank down, "No! No! The criminal on the loose! Not you!" Luke heard screaming but knew that the blood was telling the story to him. Innocent blood always screams and never stops.

At the noise Peter came running downstairs clad only in pajama bottoms.

"My God! My God, not Oscar!" And he bellowed laments in tones worthy of the biblical prophets.

Peter threw himself down and rubbed first one cheek in Oscar's still warm blood and then the other cheek until red, red blood ran all over his face and dripped down his chest and arms and hands. And the tears of Peter mixed with the blood of Oscar while distant sirens rang out the word of the death of the singing homeless man.

Later, the police came and initial reports were made. "I don't know anything, officer," Peter said softly again. "A well-beloved man, living as a kind of caretaker here, known to all as very kind. I think the only probable motive would be an unsuccessful robbery. Maybe the burglar meant to put the hammer through the window and accidentally hit his head."

---

1. J. Fred Coots/ Henry Gillespie, "Santa Claus Is Comin To Town," 1932.

Luke leaned against the wall, eyes staring at the floor, wanting to clean up Oscar's innards, still swimming around being photographed as evidence. With a blank stare, Peter looked steadily at the police and then murmured, "We are a small and quiet religious community known for our quality education."

The large policeman yawned and said, "Could it be you have an enemy from the homeless community that you serve?"

Peter waited and only shook his head yes. "Could be." He opened his mouth to say something, and then, checking his impulse, he closed his mouth.

As he left, the policeman said over his shoulder, "We will search for the next of kin but it will be difficult finding those related to this singing wonder." He walked out sadly humming, "I'm just a poor wayfaring stranger, a traveling through this world of woe."

The rosy-fingered dawn came up the next morning without the sound of Oscar's cheerful "Morning Has Broken!" Peter sat quietly in his office and barely acknowledged the presence of Jerry and Luke as they walked in, bearing an awkward tension.

Finally Peter looked up and spoke. "You will preach at Oscar's funeral, Jerry."

Raising his eyebrows, Jerry remonstrated, "Me? I barely knew him."

Peter responded, "So much the better."

"But your friendship?"

Peter jumped up, pushing the chair over behind him. "Back off from me, Jerry! Don't push me too far." And he walked out, slamming the door behind him, the walls momentarily jerking.

The day of the funeral brought a crowded church. Media trucks laden with tall ladders extending the reach of the cameras hung around hoping to catch a clue about the murder, but most worshipers were those who had known the gentle Oscar and his songs.

Clad in a medieval black robe and stole, Jerry slowly ascended in to the pulpit. "We are fools for the sake of Christ as Corinthians 4:10 says. Oscar was our fool. I claim this name for him in reverence. In the Scriptures, even King David dresses as a fool to be disguised from his own enemies. In the New Testament, fools recognized Jesus Christ as the Son of God. Oscar was our fool for the sake of Christ, the one who loved us and sang us his wisdom."

Jerry stopped and hot words came blurting out. "Our Fool of Washington, DC has been murdered and I believe one of you knows who did this outrageous monstrosity." Instantly, many looked around: is it I?

For years afterward, no one could recall what Father Jerry said next in his sermon, for the "Is it I?" sense grew and grew until some felt like Christ himself walked among them and said, "One of you will betray me." But others of less spiritual ilk explained this as too much fervent emotion and why not? At what funeral before had people ever sung "Sometimes I feel like motherless child!" accompanied by the low, moaning sobs of the slumped-over Father Peter?

Chapter Fourteen

What happens when a priest falls? No more honor for the ways of
Christ and now Lucifer exults in his domination. Priests falling into the
abyss open this sad door for others. All creation cries out for this new
betrayal of Christ, the living Son of God.

Oscar murdered and buried and still no justice. Luke walked
through the basement entrance into the basilica in northeast
Washington, the shrine devoted to the Holy Mother, the Virgin
Mary. His torn-up psyche needed the spiritual promise of a cathedral. Did God even care about this horror encompassing his life?
Walking in, Luke noticed the bookstore (no hope there because
few books are written about what you do when you discover you
have a predator bishop) and past the cafeteria (without an appetite
he couldn't even eat normally anymore.)

Then Luke saw the irritating nun from St. Charles School
eating a piece of lemon meringue pie. Maybe this would take his
mind off this problem. He walked into the dusky-dark basement
cafeteria adorned with stained glass images of the Last Supper
placed on the dark brown walls.

"Sister Clotilde, how is everything? Can I join you?"

Her head jerked up to see who spoke and then he saw worry
clenching every muscle in her face.

"Is it school? Is something wrong?"

She looked away. He saw her neck muscles tense as she swallowed.

"There are a lot of troubled thirteen- and fourteen-year-olds at school now. Do sit down, Father Luke." As she pushed the pie around with her fork, she continued, "It might just be gossip, Father, but I hear some adult is hitting on one of the seventh-grade boys. And I can't sleep anymore thinking of the damage being done to these kids. Only a kid and that poor kid is a sexual target." And burying her face in her hands, Clotilde quietly wept, her shoulders shaking.

Luke looked at the remains of the yellow pudding and the pie crust and the crappy little paper plate and he wanted to pick up the whole thing and splatter it against the ridiculously weird wall and then take that bastard bishop and rub his stupid little eyes into the yellow pudding until he yelled for mercy and then . . . Stop, Luke, stop. "Sister Clotilde, I'm going to pray. I know. I know."

Clotilde sighed and wept more as Luke walked away. She had watched him for so many years as his momentary passions flitted in and out of his life, like so many sparrows streaking across the sky and then gone forever. Her tears dripped into the lemon filling and tough crust. Their chef blended the crust too long inadvertently flitted through her trained mind.

Clotilde jumped: how did I get to be a crazy old woman crying alone in public? She saw the security guard looking at her with obvious pity: a nice-looking young man with a spiffy badge, an official hat, and a natty dark blue uniform protecting the public safety now witnessed her melt-down.

Public safety, and with that phrase Clotilde sat up straighter. That's what I do at St. Charles School. I represent public safety.

And then she knew. *Or at least that's what I pretend to do. I look in Spiderman backpacks and have never confiscated anything except a suspicious glue tube.*

What had she heard on WTOP, her news and weather radio station? The FBI had a public announcement about where to go about the abused children.

Clotilde lumbered to her feet with her extra twenty pounds around her middle bothering her, but in her eye was the committed look of a United States Marine.

"I am the incarnation of public safety and I *will* get help."

At the nunnery, she reached for her landline phone.

"Son, I need a Zipcar, you know those cute little cars parked in public spaces that you can rent for a day."

He sighed. How had this bewildered old lady found the Zipcar phone number and then felt the need to describe the cars to him? But he answered, "Sure. Credit card number please."

"No, I don't have a credit card. I'll bring you cash."

As she spoke, Clotilde was looking for her box of private money that she had hidden from the nunnery for years. A dollar here saved from a meal and a dollar there and her box was nearly full after a lifetime of service.

"No can do," came the quick response.

Taking a deep breath, she said, "Son, I am on official business for the Franciscan Sisters. I am Clotilde Kaluta who is . . ." She paused searching for the right words. "I am the Director of Public Safety." And saying this, for the first time in her life, Clotilde experienced a rush of identity. She finally knew who she was: Sister Clotilde had come into being.

"Sister Clotilde? Not the one who searched my Robin Hood backpack every day at St. Charles?" flew out the surprised answer.

"The same," she announced.

"Come into our office the day you need the Zipcar, the cute little ones parked in public spaces, and I'll put it on my credit card and you will have your Zipcar."

He paused awkwardly.

"By the way, do you know how to drive?"

But Sister Clotilde had already hung up and was headed to her crowded closet to find her shoebox full of saved money.

Let me see, he pondered. Sister Clotilde would enjoy a bright red Kia; let me arrange that for this sweet nun.

Clotilde strode into the Zipcar office and seeing the young man made eye contact.

"I am driving out to Manassas, Virginia. How much do these little contraptions cost and how do I get there?"

His hands briefly shook and then, swallowing hard, he reached for the key for the bright red new car they had just gotten in.

"You go down Route 66 for about twenty miles. Do you know where the entrance is?

The Director of Public Safety shot back, "Tell me quickly. I am on official and important business."

After explaining the directions, he stopped, "Do you want me to drive you, Sister Clotilde? We could go tomorrow."

"No. This is top secret also. I want the key now." And her gait as she headed toward the door was a mixture of a waddle and a strut.

He smiled. Somehow this was going to be all right.

Sister Clotilde pulled onto Route 66 into the right lane and started going her brisk 45 miles an hour heading toward her encounter with her new identity. Soon she adjusted to the sound of loud, beeping horns and the sight of cars swerving around her and peacefully kept the speedometer steadily fixed on her constant rate of speed.

Soon she saw signs announcing the Manassas battlefield and she knew she was getting close. Keeping her hands exactly on the same place on the steering wheel, she turned, exited, and went by the peaceful battlefield where so many young men had died, and soon saw a parking lot and chose a place far away from the door. She did not want to return this beautiful new car with its color signifying the Holy Spirit with scratches on it: red the color of blood, red the color of Christ's passion, and red the color of martyrs.

Clotilde saw the box-like building bereft of windows and saw the door. As she exited her car, she tripped on her full, ankle-length black habit, swept her full headdress back and lumbered toward the door, feeling like a wounded animal seeking relief from someone else.

Let the confrontation begin with the receptionist.

"Young man, I need help about endangered children."

The intern looked around for his supervisor who had stepped out for lunch.

"Uhh, do you have an appointment?"

Intently peering at him, she queried, "How old are you? Did you go to St. Charles School?"

"I am twenty and no, I did not." Then flushing, the thought sputtered through his mind, *why did I tell her anything?*

She continued, "This is the FBI building where they help endangered children, isn't it?"

Her authority successfully connected again.

He lamely answered, "We call them exploited children."

Clotilde knew her postmodern vocabulary. "Whatever. I want to talk to the main agent here today on official business for the Franciscan Sisters."

His hands fluttered over his computer screen and finally he uttered the fateful words, "Please sit down and I will see what I can do."

"I won't leave until I can talk to someone."

And sitting down on the one small plastic chair in the sparse room, she took out her rosary and whispered, "Hail Mary, Full of Grace, the Lord is with thee!"

He stared at her. Where was his supervisor? Maybe at a working lunch.

Two hours later, Clotilde said again, "Young man, I have finished my rosary four times over with the beads that the pope blessed. I will either have to apply for a job here or keep on praying. And the Holy Mother is getting besieged by my prayers. You are the FBI, right? We have bad things going on at St. Charles Parish and I won't leave until I talk to someone."

She muttered partly to herself, "And all these priests do about these problems is to start going on lots of picnics in the parks. We have maps of parks everywhere."

The intern sat up straighter—he had heard something about this on the news as well as in the halls here.

"Run that by me again."

"My rosary was blessed by the pope?"

He cleared his throat, hoping that he had not misheard her. "No, did you say picnics?"

"Who cares about these picnics in the parks? "

But the receptionist did not even bother answering but called an agent.

"Sir, I suggest you talk to her; it might be important."

"Son, I pray my blessings on this talk."

Then Dan walked out, sighing, but stopped when he saw the black-clothed nun. Not more prayers, thought Dan. What a waste of time. Annie, forgive me.

"I can give you five minutes," he said.

Clotilde swept into his office and did not miss a beat. "St. Charles has gone to the dogs and I want to report it."

He sat, not moving.

"Take out some paper, Mr. Anonymous FBI Agent. Write this down."

Sighing, but almost against his will, Dan reached for a notebook.

"Ignatius specifies lists, son. Number one, there is some priest after a young teenage boy. At St. Charles they think I am too old to watch and listen. I may be an old nun but I see everything. It is a gift of the Spirit."

Dan's hands started uncontrollably shaking.

"Yet all these leaders at St. Charles do is have picnics. Different parks all over the city. And they bring in outsiders—I know because they pass addresses and maps around. They should be helping these kids."

Dan reached over and pushed the buzzer under his desk. "Alert here. I need help to listen."

And into his mind he saw his wife, beautiful and young, holding Melora in Sibley Hospital, smiling even with her pale face. "We can handle her, Dan, and she will have a wonderful life!"

Maybe, Annie, maybe.

Soon a group of focused FBI agents marched in.

"Tell us everything you know, Sister."

"A kid is being targeted. And all these priests do is go to parks."

Dan muttered, "Let's find a safe house for this nun."

Laughing, Clotilde remonstrated, "But I haven't told you what is happening. They think I have dementia. I am the only safe one. That Father Luke and Jerry—they are the ones who need a safe house." She coughed and gasped, "Son. Sorry to slow you down. I know you need my help. My Lady is showing me what to do."

Then after a quick "Hail, Mary, full of grace," the whole rancid story fell out of the wizard-like nun.

And in Washington, DC, Eric wrote and translated it into texting language: "Wait, Aunt Hannah. A special agent just showed up and said they had received additional information and they want to talk to me. Do you know anything that would help me understand this?"

wait aunt hannah. special agent is here & found stuff, wants 2 tlk 2 me. Help!!

Hannah wrote and translated into texting language, "Something is up with Father Luke's group of priests. They stalk around here like lively stallions and quite frankly, it is good to see them acting this way! Not the dull, lifeless group they used to be."

something weird w/ father Luke clique :/ so enthusiastic! used 2 b zombies.

Luke headed to the basin of holy water. Crossing himself, head down, he started walking towards the parking lot. His cell phone vibrated, and then grabbing it, he saw a Virginia number. He answered mechanically, "Father Luke here."

"Special agent Dan Miller here from the FBI unit in Manassas, Virginia."

And Luke felt relief flowing through every atom of his body. Could help come from here?

Dan began with, "That's some nun you got." He paused while Luke gasped and then continued. "Eric gave me your number. We need to talk. I've seen the pictures of the kids. Tell me about the parks."

Chapter Fifteen

What happens when a priest falls? Others, feeling the vicious attack, cry out for Christ's grace and love. Mary weeps and prays.

Luke walked into the FBI office. Running through his mind was the mantra from the prophet stationed by himself in front of the Vatican embassy: *"You don't need this bishop to tell you what to do."*

Special Agent Dan handed some pictures across to Luke. "Recognize any kids?"

Luke saw the first picture of the boy, his shirt pushed suggestively aside. "That's Andrew."

Another boy showed up next. "Unfortunately I can't identify him." A young woman dressed in a bikini. "That's a new teacher."

Luke spoke, "It takes a mystic to understand one. The bishop wants completeness and wholeness and is convinced that in his sexual acts he is becoming one with the universe and one with God. He looks around the room of priests and thinks that when he has dominated all of them, then the mystery of God appears."

Dan frowned.

"For Cahill the prostitutes are merely the warm-up act for sex that brings full revelation of God. Occult mysteries we call them."

Apocalypse now. The tottering world of human dignity and standards had fallen into utter chaos only identifiable by the human lusts of Bishop Cahill and Father Leo. And lust tore down the wholesome boundaries constructed by the Spirit and only a burned-out hulk remained of Saint Peter the Fisherman's Roman Catholic Church.

Finally Luke's shaking hands reached the end of the pictures. He exploded, "How do they get away with all of this?"

Dan stopped. "Have you never heard of the Dark Web? Or Deep Web?"

Luke, staring at his lap, only muttered. "No."

"Most of the Internet now is taken up with the criminal activity on the secret Dark Web. You can buy anything there: humans, pornography, guns, weapons. And buy them anonymously."

Luke sighed deeply. Then looking up he saw in the special agent's eyes the look of moral outrage that Luke had always yearned to see in the eyes of the corrupt Bishop Cahill.

For days Peter had sat at his desk looking out the window, as if waiting for the cheerful sight of Oscar coming home. His limp body barely moving, Peter seemed like a vacant house. A stream of somber parishioners brought in ham and cheese sandwiches, egg salad sandwiches, and strawberry tarts, but the untouched food began to clutter up his office and every evening Carlos methodically threw it out.

Returning from his appointment, Luke was walking by his office and Peter called him in.

Abruptly Peter began, "Don't play dumb with me, Luke. I know that you know what's happened here." Peter ignored the tears streaming from his eyes. "I see that I inadvertently murdered my only friend. Didn't I? Wouldn't Ignatius say that?"

Luke paused. Then he spoke calmly, "Discerning the spirits, Father, is a complicated business."

Peter vociferated, "You idiot! I don't want your priest games. I want the truth. Can't you see? I wanted God but played with sex on the side and pictures that excited me to do this. No big deal, right? But then Leo came and he was into much worse spirits but the same genre. He began the practice of orgies, and meetings in playgrounds. And one evening, Luke, I went to the playground to meet some prostitutes and Oscar followed me. He was probably humming and singing "I want to be ready to walk in Jerusalem!" And when I approached the wrong person, Oscar helped me after I was beaten. And Leo said, "Tell everyone the propositioning priest was Luke." And you were probably one of the few celibate priests around. And I did it to your reputation and I didn't care. As long as my friend Oscar and I were together, I was fine. But Leo knew Oscar saw the whole thing and took over and ordered his murder. Oscar, Oscar, if I only knew what I was doing." And struggling not to, Peter gave way to sobbing, shielding the sight of his eyes with two uplifted hands.

"Who knocked his brains out? I was sleeping on my job, day and night, and now I know that I killed the only person I loved." Peter held his head in his hands and sobbed, "My friend, my friend."

And Luke walked over and kneeling put his arms around the sobbing man. Then Peter pushed him away.

"Get me a phone number." Peter sat down and began his letter to the authorities, his strange life's opus. His letter ended, "Oscar, thee will I cherish, thee will I honor, until I find your killer and get rid of the predator Bishop Cahill." Oscar's voice seemed to sing and echo around the words as Peter wrote it.

Dan sat in his office, waiting for this man, a big fish in the Roman Catholic Church, and soon he saw the elegant Monsignor Peter, completely dressed in a black liturgical surplice with a prominent gold and jeweled cross displayed on his chest, proceeding regally into the FBI building. Dan received his first big clue: the monsignor was not afraid of being recognized here and would be a formidable enemy to any who got in the way of justice for Oscar.

Taking an authoritative role, the now-galvanized Peter sat across from Dan and began.

"What do you need to know to get these people?"

Dan responded, "Their inner workings: what they are into, sex chat rooms? Kid porn? Prostitution?" Dan added, "And now it might be murder."

Peter flinched but kept his direct gaze. "I'll tell you everything I know."

Dan pushed back. "Why are you talking?

"I want revenge." Peter looked away for a second, then added "What I say will surprise you."

Dan half-smiled. "I can take it."

"Okay, then. My deal is I will tell you everything but I want Leo caught, arrested, and incarcerated for the murder of Oscar. That is what I want. "

"I'll do what I can but of course I make no promise. Let's start."

Peter began his story. "It all comes from Bishop Cahill. He is a sexual predator requiring sexual relations with every priest and seminarian that works for him. I was one of them. He was my first sexual partner and demanded this of me. And I went along and became a monsignor out of it.

"My conscience was screaming at me that this is wrong, but I needed and wanted this promotion. "The lust of the flesh against the spirit," Saint Paul called it. I was a slave to this. I wanted to be the monsignor."

Dan knew he had found the person he needed.

"I only found out later that Cahill and Leo were into crimes." He looked out the window. "I know my moral theology. If I don't do what I can, then I am guilty of harming these people too."

The agent leaned forward. "Let's get these people off the streets." Then Dan continued, "What was Oscar singing before he was murdered?"

"I think it was *List to the mocking bird*. He did not say listen but list. And then his final song, *Up on the housetop, reindeer paws.*""

Dan thought through the song. "The words could mean, The mockingbird is making a list and someone is on the housetop.

Coincidence, Monsignor? Did he know about the diocesan list? Could he be saying that the mocking bishop was making a list?"

Peter slumped over again. "Oscar seemed to know everything. I surely wish . . ."

"You've done the right thing now."

"I need to know if Cahill and Leo suspect anything?"

"No, of course not, and they would not worry even if they knew. Any films they make go straight to some sort of organized crime network. Cahill and Leo are into as many victims as they can: filmed or not, just as long as they exercise domination."

In his St. Charles office, Leo sat back and stared at the wall—how to pull Andrew's seduction off? The texts clang in and out "ofc u like this!" with pictures of male and female private parts.

Then guessing, "Ash's hair might be grt."

"Share this with ppl!"

More sexting.

Andrew turned his cell phone on to vibrate and between classes ran to the bathroom to look.

Wow! What a cool priest. Father Leo understood his love for Ashley.

Chapter Sixteen

What happens when a priest falls? Yet a new way opens. Will anyone go this way of living holiness?

On the Potomac River tidal basin, the pink cherry blossoms drooped over and surrounded the strolling people, with the flowers looking like lusciously light rose tinted whipped cream ravishing all senses with their delicate aroma and universal beauty. Japanese, French, German, Spanish, Korean, and other languages all blended together and tourists from around the world united in a huge cloud of sublime ecstasy, a vision of heaven where all shall be one. Couples slowly paddled around the Tidal Basin, chatting of this and that, while admiring the memorial to Thomas Jefferson and his principles of freedom.

Father Leo left his Maundy Thursday Holy Week service and bought an extra-frothy cappuccino from a vendor and waited for his weekly phone call from his contact in the Vatican.

"Perfect timing! Enjoy this new convert right before the celebration of Good Friday and Easter. I'll wait my turn while the bishop initiates him into our select group." Chills ran up and down his spine. How many pinwheels will we put in the tree tonight?

It was at cherry blossom time when many rendezvous happened and Leo hoped for more and more flamboyant actions this time of year. He knew it was time of testing: his first Cherry

Blossom Festival; what exploits could he pull off? Letting his imagination run wild, Leo knew he was up for the task.

In the Cherry Blossom Parade, the bass drum from Wilson High School Marching Band boomed block after block. The piccolo whistled the Capitol Hill composer John Philips Sousa's "The Washington Post March." And Andrew started his walk toward West Potomac Park, slowly, tentatively. As he moved through the haze of pink cherry blossoms, he reflected on his good SAT scores, along with his good grades, and now he wanted to know what it was like to make out with a girl and not any girl, but Ashley. They must have invited all the kids and Andrew thought that sneaking away with all these low-hanging cherry blossoms would be easy and kissing in all this beauty would be natural.

The singer on the platform near the sublimely beautiful cherry blossoms sang out Stephen Foster's "I Dream of Jeannie with the Light Brown Hair." Marching by on Constitution Avenue, lithe girls strutted by in shiny and garish pink and red satin dresses swirling around, flashing huge banners with cherry blossoms enflamed on that announced the end of innocence. Writhing exotic dancers in bars looked at patrons with contempt, while new red drinks with colored vodka enflamed the passion to become one with the cherry blossoms.

Back at the Manassas FBI building, Dan asked Peter, "What significance does the pinwheel have?'

"I don't know. I have racked my brain and I don't know."

Then Peter pondered on this while driving home. Stanton Park, Georgetown Park, Anacostia Park. They sound like the spokes of wheel. Like the actual layout of DC, but no not a wheel, a pinwheel. If a pinwheel was put on a map of DC, we might see the pattern of the bishop's attacks.

Reaching the office, he grabbed the map of DC and started jotting in a pinwheel. That's it! But does he go symmetrically or not? He tried it one way and then another.

Finally he got something that looked like a pinwheel resting on the DC map and Peter could see Cahill's vision for the pinwheel claiming the spiritual power of Washington DC. Put blood in every park and we own Washington, DC.

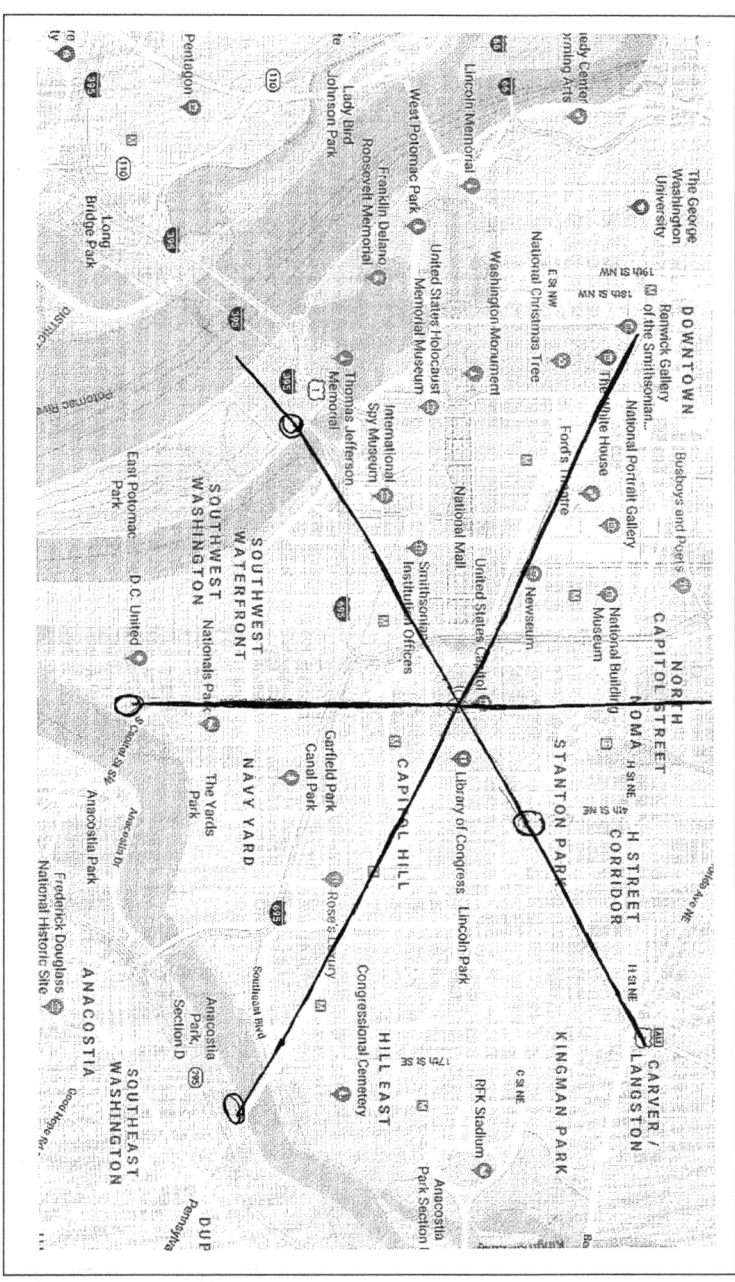

In the pinwheel shape, Stanton Park resided in the center. A ray extended up to Mount Vernon Park near the DC Convention Center; a ray extending down through Buzzard's Point; a ray extending to the side through Anacostia Park. So what remained for the fulfillment of this spiritual claiming was northwest up or southwest down. Hands trembling, Peter sketched in a ray each direction and saw two or three possible parks that remained for the bishop's crimes. So close to the epicenter of this havoc, Peter broke out in a sweat.

Suddenly the phone broke the silence, ringing, ringing, ringing. It started screeching. Finally Peter grabbed it as he continued to scan the map only to hear Annette's shrill voice yelling, "Peter—help! It's Andrew. He's headed to a park to meet Leo and someone else. I don't know which park."

Peter answered quickly, "How do you know?"

"He dropped his iPhone when he was leaving and on the first page he had four texts with sex pictures on it from Leo. Good God! What have we done? We've got to stop him or something awful will happen."

"Do the texts say which park?"

"Leo mentions meeting at a willow tree. Andrew's phone is under a password I don't know. These are all the texts I can see on the front."

"Let me go talk to Luke. See if you can remember any clues about parks lately."

Sprinting down the hall, Peter banged on Luke's door. He looked intently into his eyes and rapidly announced, "I think we have the pattern of attacks. Come look. Quick. Andrew's in danger."

Sprinting back to the office, Luke's scanned quickly Peter's map.

Peter pointed. "Bishop seems to be ready to move into northwest or southwest DC." Sweat broke out on his forehead.

Watching and alert, Luke said. "We'll go to West Potomac in southwest DC; it's large and we can cover different territory. Let's get Jerry and Hannah to go to Guy Mason Park, near the vice president's residence in northwest DC. You call Dan and tell him what we are doing." Coolly, Luke texted Jerry. "Emergency! Stop Andrew from meeting bish. Chck Guy Mason park right away." Then Luke stopped wondering how do you text the word "tragedy"? Then he texted every letter.

"Potential tragedy. Help!"

In the glories of the dark spring evening, Leo opened the bishop's car door.

"There," he said pointing. "Underneath the huge willow tree down a short way from the cherry blossoms. It will be dark and private and a great place to become the mentor for this young man with all those long willow branches surrounding you all. Andrew will make a great priest one day under your tutelage. What a great service you are doing for the church!"

The bishop strode over to the immense weeping tree and waited. Ahh, what a moment! Another convert to his priesthood.

The bishop took out the pocket knife given to him by the Vatican. He stepped back, raised the knife over his head and swishing it hit the tree with all his strength and broke back the bark into the tree's tender interior. He twisted and turned it and with sap swelling out, mutilated the bark in six different directions until the shape of a pinwheel hung on the surface like graffiti announcing chaos.

And soon he saw the young boy walking slowly along the cherry blossom path, head cocked, scanning the horizon.

"Over here, Andrew!" Cahill yelled.

"Where are the kids? I mean, bishop, I thought there were other kids here for some picnic."

"They're on their way, my son. Come and wait with me. We can talk of your career and maybe you will be like me, a faithful priest in our Roman church."

Hannah and Jerry sped off to Guy Mason Park in Georgetown. Turning onto northwest K Street, Jerry found crowded lanes of traffic with this tourist season in Washington, DC, but zipping around cars and alertly watching for pedestrians wearing telltale pink shirts with blossoms on them, he made it to 23rd and K Street. Suddenly the sound of sirens and the sight of speeding black suburban SUVs surrounding seven black limousines appeared from the vicinity of the White House. Authoritative police zoomed out of nowhere on motorcycles and stopped all traffic. Far-away sirens clinched the deal that they were dead in the water as far as approaching Georgetown.

Jerry hit the steering wheel. "Damn! What now? Any news from Luke?"

Quickly checking her phone, Hannah responded, "No but this traffic jam must be related to the IMF meeting. They are probably having a dinner party and we are stopped for their security. But if we're having trouble, the bishop will also. This makes more likely it is the Tidal Basin near the Cherry Blossoms."

And Hannah texted, "Leaving Grtwn. IMF trfk. To Tdal Bsn soon."

And Jerry, still in his collar, got out of the car and yelled at the motorcycle policeman, "I am on my way to an emergency. Let me turn around."

The police looked at him and shook his head no. "No one is moving, buddy. We have the leaders of Italy coming through."

Then Jerry, seeing with inner eyes the strength of the nurturing wolf, pleaded, "In the name of God, let us pass!"

And the Catholic police looked left, right, behind and in front: no sign of his supervisor.

He walked over and announced loudly, "K Street is closed." Then he leaned over and whispered, "I did not tell you this but look. The alley is still open."

And Jerry grabbed his hand and jumped back in the car. He did an illegal U-turn, drove too fast through the alley block after block and soon saw the welcoming sight of Independence Ave where he turned right and headed to the Tidal Basin.

Driving too fast, Luke had already reached the Tidal Basin. Near the paddleboat concession stand, he deserted the car and started running toward West Potomac looking for willow trees, so many nestled on the moist banks of the flowing river.

Luke saw movement and heard muted sounds from a tree and began sprinting toward a willow tree—anything to stop this crime! No! This cannot happen! As he sprinted towards the Potomac River, Leo stepped out and blocked Luke's way by his muscular arms.

"Don't get involved here, Padre," he said mockingly. He quickly twisted Luke's arm behind his back. But Luke was beyond care for his own protection and as Leo pushed him down, he started his full-throated screams, "Leave Andrew alone! You are priests! Stop this insanity!"

Leo kicked his foot into Luke's mouth, kicking out one of his front teeth. As the blood spurted from the open wounds, Luke heard ringing while feeling bathed in his own fresh blood. Leo continued kicking in his stomach and groin until Luke lay limp with agony. He twisted some to try to avoid the continuing attacks but soon all efforts to relieve the pain ended.

Leo quietly taunted, "Shut up, you fool! Don't you know that these are the perks? Who cares about a few kids here or there?" In a taunting voice, he continued, "We carry the church triumphant."

The larger Leo dragged him to the banks of the Potomac River and, throwing Luke into the shallow water, Leo ran off, deserting the bizarre scene.

As the pain raged through his body, Luke felt an invitation coming from the wide and peaceful river, to leave all this chaos behind and float off to become one with the deep, flowing water. Then suddenly he felt someone sitting next to him and gazing over the wide river. Why, it looked like a man from a different time and it seemed to be Saint Ignatius. Luke thought for a second he was losing his mind as well as his teeth, but the comfort from this man's presence flowed all over him and he yielded to this consolation.

Ignatius sat on a fallen, submerged tree, his feet resting in the flowing water, and smiled at Father Luke.

"*What a soldier you are,*" Ignatius said softly, his voice echoing over the water. "*No commanding officer except for me. No army except a fallen Baptist administrator and her agnostic nephew and a few other priests and one hopeful Jesuit. And finally Peter joined with you, an awakened, sinful priest.*

"Let me draw this together for you. Someone will find you sooner or later. With friends like Hannah and Eric, you won't be forgotten forever. This doesn't mean you won't suffer here. Your mouth is not a pretty sight. But in your suffering, you will find purification and avoid the pains of purgatory and the screams of the damned from hell. Hell is real, Father Luke, very, very real.

"I see your yearning for death. Remember the spiritual exercises: if you are strong enough, tell God to use you as God wills, not as expedient or good for you. If you are not strong enough, and only you know that, then scream for mercy to God."

Ignatius looked at Luke. *"Let me tell you a story about my life. I was an excellent warrior, a real one. When I was injured, I spent almost a year recuperating and no one thought I would really survive. But I did because I really wanted to have enough time to be part of the only war that only counts: the war against evil. You know this war and you have been a noble fighter to set this right."* Ignatius seemed to listen for a second. *"Those people looking for a cheap thrill; they've missed all of life. But they aren't to be ignored; through them comes the corruption of the human race. You found the inner energy to fight, Luke. You found life at its deepest and most profound level."* Luke rested, surrounded by a deep sense of serenity.

Ignatius sat gently, *"Live, Luke! You are very much needed. You have more battles to fight and I have more wisdom to give you."*

Near the Jefferson Memorial, Hannah and Jerry arrived in the park area. Hannah repeated, "What had the last text said: something about a willow tree near the cherry blossoms."

Jerry chose quickly. "Let me head over to the Washington Monument, you go past the Jefferson Memorial." Quickly agreeing, they separated.

Alert Hannah jogged over near the Jefferson Memorial, trying to run from tree to tree. She tried to listen and heard a door slamming. Instinctively, she looked for a light but it was dark.

She heard odd thuds from the end of West Potomac Park, but still too far for her to reach soon. Then out of the corner of her eye she saw an Emergency Call alarm in the deserted area, placed there for distressed joggers. What else could she do? The sexting to Andrew about the willow tree jangled in her mind like a knife stabbing in her heart. Then she reached out for the emergency alarm and pulled the red lever down, breaking glass and releasing the welcome sound of clanging bells. Hannah stopped, though her feet wanted to continue running. Better wait here where the police could locate her.

She heard yelling along with the sound of running feet and curses. "Shit! Who did that?"

Hannah ran out to the street, scanning the horizon and soon she saw a shadow slowly coming around the corner. Then she saw the middle-aged policemen struggling his way over, pedaling quickly on his bicycle, and in the distance the sound of a Washington, DC fire engine behind him approaching for support.

And to her surprise Hannah yelled in her loudest voice, "Come and arrest these devils!" Then in a louder voice she screamed, "Come quick! Big fire!" Energized, one of the few policeman not guarding IMF leaders revolved his feet faster and the bicycle carrying help arrived for Andrew in the midst of the dark night of Washington, DC.

Then sounds of loud voices yelling came from a whizzing car, "FBI! Don't try to get out."

He heard Cahill's frantic voice, "Who called the police? This is a private religious ceremony."

And Dan came bursting in screaming, "Stop where you are!" And then in a burst of noise, "You were the bastard in the movie with the teenager!" And Bishop Cahill turned and faced Dan, who raised and aimed his gun at him.

Andrew ran out with bruised and reddened welts rising on his face. His shirt hung with expertly cut ends and his glazed eyes looked around in shock. Without taking his eyes off the bishop, Dan ordered, "Get him in the ambulance! Tell the hospital to get evidence."

Then softly, "You okay, son? Did he harm you?"

Then Andrew hung his head. "No but he was trying." In a clogged voice, he said, "I was fighting."

"This is not your fault. You hear me: this is not your fault." Then Dan gestured, "You carry yourself over to the ambulance. You are a strong kid and this is going to be fine. We will let your mother know you are at the Georgetown Hospital. And don't be afraid: you will not be blamed for this."

As Andrew walked toward the revolving red light, Cahill yelled, "I am doing this all for Christ!" He took his Vatican knife out and pointed it directly at his chest.

Dan aimed his gun directly at the bishop.

Jumping out of the car from behind Dan, Peter stepped forward and placing a cautionary hand behind his back, signaling others to stay away. The tree's mutilated bark already showed the sign of a pinwheel.

Then in a sympathetic voice, Peter reassured the bishop, "Bishop, of course you are. You are only concerned about being a good pastor. I understand that. But the pinwheel? I don't understand the pinwheel and to complete your great legacy could you explain this to me?"

Cahill looked toward his former protégé. "I am claiming this powerful city for Christ. Dear son, the Greek letters for Christ piled on top of each other, of course. Don't you know that? As ancient a symbol as the fish, the ichthus they called it. Every person initiated into this great tribe remembered by the ichthus."

In an affectionate tone, Peter continued, "Hey, let me see that knife. You know, I think I have one just like that that I got in Rome."

The bishop handed him the knife, while the police grabbed Cahill from behind.

Dan muttered, "Read him his rights, book him, and take him to the DC jail."

Still in the river, Luke saw deep darkness that he had never even known existed and now he made out the shape of a wolf sitting near him. What was that? Was he already dead? Luke knew not in which world he dwelt.

Near the river's lapping water, Ignatius smiled at Luke. "*Ready to join in the fray? They got the dreadful bishop and he will spend the rest of his days in prison.*"

Luke grimaced as he tried to speak, "I don't know if I am up for this anymore. Maybe my time should end now."

Luke took his weak hand and started caressing the alluring water and watched the sweet ripples forming on the river.

Ignatius leaned over, "*No, Luke, no. This will be the interesting time. Understand evil and God and love. See what else you can do. Don't decide life is too difficult now. Life sprints by and you want to fight as much as you can.*"

Luke tried to focus his eyes, and saw on the beach the she-wolf patiently waiting. Her eyes fixed not on Ignatius, but she looked deeply into Luke's eyes. With their eye-to-eye, heart-to-heart, and soul-to-soul connections, the pure raw power of life flowed between them. Her deep eyes showed deep compassion. Then the she-wolf lifted her long snout back, looked at the sky and howled: loud and courageous and sweet. Luke heard in her unearthly melody a tale of perseverance and survival; of the glories of the fights and the battles and the divine war. The she-wolf stopped and looked at him again.

So Luke, disoriented from his loss of blood, started moaning himself and splashing the cool river water with his hand. Then even a short howl erupted from his dangerously weakened body. Dan heard and ordered another agent, "A victim in the river. Get help right away." Soon, with bells tolling, ambulances arrived and they carried Luke to the fifth floor ICU of the Georgetown University Hospital.

Leo started backing off, keeping his eyes on the police car's flashing lights. Red—the color of dripping blood banged on the trees and pavement. *Blood danger* screamed out the lights. Then turning he ran—his legs thrown out like a thoroughbred horse, breaking all boundaries—and lunging for safety—or is there ever any safety? The running Leo reached his car. He hit the starter. *Where to go?* Haines Point dropped in his mind like a waiting friend. *My friends from the parties are there. Look at the cars. No running red lights or stop signs.* He grabbed his Roman collar and threw it out the window. *I don't want to be connected with them. Collar did not hit anyone, no throwing missile charges. I've spent my whole life dodging the law and the prophets. Now is not the time to get caught. Relief—I need relief.*

He exhaled when he saw the sign for Ohio Avenue. Red cherry blossoms parking lots. The blood danger had passed. After a brief paid encounter, Leo straightened his hair. He reached into his inner pocket where with shaking hand, he felt his passport. Breathing out, Leo knew his friends in Rome would protect him.

Judgment. No one escapes judgment. I need to get to the airport. Passport in hand, Leo disappeared through the shiny doors of Ronald Reagan International Airport.

Chapter Seventeen

What happens when a priest falls? They have reached for endless ecstasy and found eternal corruption. All creation sings the lament of the dying soul. Yet this dirge of death may awaken the hearts of faithful ones. As Oscar sang, "What wondrous love is this, O my soul?"

The next day while resting in the hospital, Luke took out his Saint Ignatius's notebook and wrote.

8. Ignatius helps us. Mary helps us. Christ helps us.

9. Deliverance is real. Be like a wolf passionate about the pack and howling to encounter one another.

David came to see Luke at Georgetown Hospital. Luke's bed was tilted up so he sat almost upright. An untouched bowl of strawberry jello sat on his tray.

"Our history together helps, Luke. You've listened to my theology before. Evil attacks with a wretched desolation. Evil leaves ugly footprints in our lives that never completely disappear."

Luke's eyes filled with anger. He aimlessly spun the red jello close to the edge of the tray.

David continued. "The desire for revenge will destroy you. Think of the footprints, Luke. Evil went face-to-face with your soul. It took away all justice and laughed at your pain."

Luke's fists unclenched some.

"The mocking, the intention to harm, the suffering. You will never forget that."

David assessed Luke's angry eyes. He continued.

"You will hate those footprints in your soul to your dying day. I am not glossing that over. It is like human beings have lost the will to live and to survive. "

David paused.

"But remember the goodness of the One who died for us. He too carried the footprints of evil and he will carry yours also."

The quiet ticking of the hospital monitors filled the room.

Suddenly Luke offered, "A couple of months ago I saw a ghost reaching out to me. On St. Charles stairs."

"That was a gift to let you know evil was there. Who knows what type of apparition? Maybe the ghost of a child victim. Evil never sneaks in without signs. That's the tragedy. Someone knows what is happening and can help. And how many kids have suffered? How many?"

More quiet.

"We can talk whenever you want."

Luke only said, "The Dark Web. We've gone into this deep and evil place."

Nodding, David's eyes filled with tears.

"Those ugly footsteps will never disappear. But think redemption, Luke, our hope of glory."

And four weeks later, leaning on Jerry, Luke hobbled toward the Vatican embassy.

The old man with the sign "Mess on Top" walked towards them. He said, "Listening to your soul now, buddy?" Then he went back to waving at friendly drivers.

Dr. Wagner walked into the subdued group of priests sitting quietly in their room in the back of the Vatican embassy. Silence reigned.

Talking slowly, Hudson began, "What I have found out has surprised me: I never believed that my church could have a predator bishop. And this is unsettling."

In simplicity, Wagner said, "Yes."

Hudson finished, "But since the bishop was arrested, an independent investigative team has been established to investigate clerical misconduct of whatever kind. There is a hotline now.

"Our new bishop tells us, "Hey, guys, this is going to be in the news and get ready for it." Last week I read about it in *USA Today.* Our diocese is starting to pay out millions in damages."

The priests passed around an article from *USA Today* with a garish picture of the smiling Bishop Cahill, Father Leo, and Monsignor Peter from last winter's Caribbean cruise. The trio stood in red-flowered shirts on the ship deck with their arms casually thrown around each other's shoulders. The title read "Bishop Charged with Sex Crimes." A subtitle read, "A Prominent Monsignor to Testify for Justice Department in Trial."

Bruce jumped in, "Now with the National Dallas Charter there is not a lot of wiggle room. Now you may be investigated unannounced 24/7, and everything can be gone through: personal clothing, computers, libraries, pictures."

Luke said quickly, "What about the kids? I hear we have not found the poor boy who left messages about the running water."

Dr. Wagner, a new father himself, got this. "It makes me sick to think of those kids." He shook his head. "That's got to be the focus."

Jerry looked at the therapist. "Right. We have a new bishop who at least talks about stopping this. After Cahill we were happy to have anyone. I mean, you cannot imagine how atrocious that was."

"I served on the council a couple of years with Bishop Cahill and some caved under his sexual pressure. We were afraid to say things."

Hudson said, "Yes, I was one of those afraid to speak until I saw Cahill firsthand. You know who is going to help now is General Knight. He saw enough to be an objective witness at the situation without knowing any of the details. This is going to be a down and dirty fight in court but he will help a lot."

"We have been living this for all these years. I think there is quite a bit of anger."

Sadly, Jerry said, "We still have a tragedy here. Leo ordered Oscar's murder and has gotten away with it."

Luke questioned, "Where would he go?"

"The Vatican, of course. He is now safely inside his Vatican group or in a place arranged for him."

Bruce jumped in, "We're dropping like flies!"

After the groans and laughter subsided, Wagner said quietly, "Peter?"

Luke spoke up, "He's in a safe house until after the trial. With Leo still missing, Peter needs protection. After the trial, who knows what will happen?"

Wagner smiled, "And Jerry, you, our Roman leader, what are you about now?"

Jerry blushed. "Hard to believe but I finally have finished my dissertation. "The Impact of the Roman Symbol of She-Wolf on the early Christian Church." And Sanchez said he would help on my dissertation committee." His eyes became red while almost inaudibly adding, "Our Lady helped me."

Nodding yes, Luke said, "Remember my line from Ignatius.

> *May Our Lady intercede between us poor sinners and her*
> *Son and Lord; may she obtain for us the grace that, with*
> *the cooperation of our own toil and effort, our weak and*
> *sorry spirits may be made strong and joyful in his praise.*[1]

The atmosphere quickened and Wagner just waited.

Luke added, "I used to say loneliness was the essence of my life. That is finished."

---

1. Ignatius of Loyola, *Spiritual Exercises*, 327.

Then Jerry stood and spoke in a grand voice while all the priests watched. "Brothers, quite true, I hope our loneliness is ended. And while our wise church hierarchy did not suspect how we would use these therapy groups, they helped bring some justice. Our Bishop Cahill is heading to prison. We are the remnant now. The faithful left behind after the first purification. There will be more fires and purifications. This is not over. After all, the blood of the martyrs is the seed of the church. We are the faithful remnant remaining after the fire of love from our Lord fell on us. What will God do with us?" And silence reigned. Could there be a divine purpose here?

Silence filled the room. Radiating beauty filled empty spiritual spaces. After the mass destruction, the remnant becomes the start of beautiful, pure growth.

Jerry continued. "I invite us to celebrate. The desert fathers and mothers knew about suffering and so do we. Now I brought Saint Mary of Egypt beans, my Saint Bruno coffee, and in honor of our founder Saint Ignatius, some lovely fruit bread made from imported Spanish fruit." Slowly the priests stood up, all except the bruised Luke.

Quiet reigned as Jerry spooned out the drink.

Jerry raised his coffee cup. "To God: Father, Son, and Holy Spirit. To Saint Ignatius.

"And to you, my dear friends, we few, we happy few, we band of brothers."

After the meal, the weary, black-clad priests found their way back to their rectories facing into new hours of busy service.

Dr. Wagner put together his final report. "Some priests express concern about the sexual abuse scandal and the effects this has had on the diocese of Washington, DC. Some mention feeling uninformed about new information concerning the sexual abuse scandal. Others mention concern about current investigations underway that seek information about the activities of certain priests. Some priests talk about Bishop Cahill and the fallout from his leadership of the diocese."

Then leaning forward and holding his hands in his head, Wagner thought, "You guys did it. I always knew you could." And for the first time, this competent therapist held his head in his hands and wept.

The following Sunday morning, Hannah made a surprise appearance in church, her long blonde braids neatly framing her glowing face.

The bandaged Luke sat on the side of the sanctuary, still too bruised to stand and participate. To his surprise, Hannah proudly walked up front and took her place by his side.

Luke waved warmly at her. "Your poor tooth," Hannah murmured. "But I bet your understanding has grown by lots. And the predator bishop is gone!"

Following the mass, Father David Sanchez walked over and handed the newly consecrated bread and wine to Luke, who wincingly swallowed some. Sanchez leaned down and whispered into Luke's ear, "Blessings upon you, Father, for letting your zeal for the Lord consume your life!" With a distant look in his eye, Sanchez looked at the saddened Luke and added, "Leo showed pornographic pictures to his acolyte who then in turn tried to pass it on down to an innocent three-year-old. You stopped it in time." He paused. "That is a very good thing you did. I want to be very clear about this."

Later that month, with the injured Luke lying in the back seat, Jerry drove Dr. Sanchez back to Dulles Airport to fly home to Rome.

Dr. Sanchez pondered, "What made this one more malevolent was Peter's ability to woo the mothers of the boys. I think this was probably some light physical involvement, maybe just kissing. But the effect was to silence the mothers and once you have taken away the voice of parents, anything can happen to the children.

"Silence the whistleblowers through threats of trumped-up charges, and silence the mothers through their own guilt of improper involvement, and the children are open targets. And the Evil One always aims at the most vulnerable of humanity, our children whom all adults should be protecting.

"In the beginning was the Word and when Lucifer takes our words away, evil rules."

Dr. Sanchez turned towards Luke. "One question is worthy of your time. What went wrong that we received the gospel so mistakenly? Ponder it. Now that you have cut your teeth and know the ways of spiritual warfare, I guarantee you that evil will challenge you again. But until that moment, focus on the gospel and the negation of it we have just lived through."

Luke blurted out, "Is it organized? A brotherhood?"

"Don't push so hard, my friend. Catch your breath for the next battle. Who knows?"

"Remember the Vatican banker found hung in Rome? And what about Moloch?"

David frowned. "Moloch is the demon of child sacrifice. Yet a warrior knows when it is time for quiet. You need to get ready for what is coming. This situation has prepared you for something else." Smiling, he added, "You remember the theological term: prevenient grace. In the economy of God, no effort is wasted. You have more battles coming, Luke."

Luke smiled, grimacing with his still sore gums. "I hope not. We won, didn't we?"

David said, "Merely the battle. Leo is missing. With his organized crime contacts, he's made it out of the country. Cahill sowed enough seeds of evil for generations of disorder and unhappiness. Evil only waits its day and bides its time. But for the moment, for only the moment, light has shone in the darkness and not overcome it."

David playfully hit Jerry in the arm and briefly hugged Luke at the airport. "See you soon." David walked through security, turned around, waved to Luke, and then visibly crossed himself. He walked towards the plane to take him back to Rome and home.

Luke pondered that maybe theology is only understood running on the fly. As they stood between crime and the church hierarchy, somehow a way opened and somehow hearts live and a new rosy-fingered day dawns. Yet the Christian faith is itself at risk now, he thought. Could we be a living remnant that God ordained and touched with gracious hands of mercy?

Luke picked up his cell phone. "Hannah," he said gently, "Are you and Eric up to having lunch? We all have a lot to talk about."

Hannah smiled. "That minister Mr. Golightly told me about this. Remnants. We are called living remnants."

Luke paused. "We might know now the living presence of God."

Quiet.

What happens when a priest falls? A journey into darkness like no other horrifies and yet, the light of God, moving in sublime living holiness, loves and strengthens those who remain. Pure and holy life calls the remnant into the renewed holiness of divine light.

Bibliography

Dimler, G. Richard. *The Jesuit Emblem*. Companion to Emblem Studies. New York: AMS, 2008.

————. *Studies in the Jesuit Emblem*. Studies in the Emblem 19. New York: AMS, 2007.

Francis. "On Care for our Common Home." May 24, 2015. http://w2.vatican.va/content/francesco/en/encyclicals/documents/papa-francesco_20150524_enciclica-laudato-si.html.

Ignatius of Loyola. *Spiritual Exercises and Selected Works*. New York: Paulist, 1991.

James, Nancy Carol. *The Apophatic Mysticism of Madame Guyon*. Ann Arbor, MI: UMI Dissertation Services, 1998.

————. *The Complete Madame Guyon*. Paraclete Giants. Orleans, MA: Paraclete, 2011.

————. *I, Jeanne Guyon*. Jacksonville, FL: SeedSowers, 2014.

————. *Jeanne Guyon's Christian Worldview*. Eugene, OR: Pickwick, 2017.

————. *The Pure Love of Madame Guyon*. Lanham, MD: University Press of America, 2007.

————. *The Soul, Lover of God: Emblems by Madame Guyon and Herman Hugo*. Lanham, MD: University Press of America, 2014.

James, William. *The Varieties of Religious Experience*. New York: Barnes & Noble Classics, 2004.